Playing for Life

Sports Stories for

Nate Aaseng

AUGSBURG Publishing House • Minneapolis

PLAYING FOR LIFE
Sports Stories for Young Teens

Copyright © 1987 Augsburg Publishing House

Photos: James J. Baron, 10, 36, 68; Bruce Klobeke, 16, 102; David S. Strickler, 28; Cheryl A. Ertelt, 50; Jean-Claude Lejeune, 72, 96; Renaud Thomas, 90.

Library of Congress Cataloging-in-Publication Data

Aaseng, Nathan.
  PLAYING FOR LIFE.

  Summary: A collection of true stories in which athletes perform acts of great kindness and caring for others.
  1. Athletes—United States—Biography—Juvenile literature.   2. Athletes—Religious life—Juvenile literature.   [1. Athletes.   2. Christian life]
I. Title.
GV697.A1A63   1987   796.092'2   [B]   [92]   87-18837
ISBN 0-8066-2279-2

Manufactured in the U.S.A.   APH 10-4997

1   2   3   4   5   6   7   8   9   0   1   2   3   4   5   6   7   8   9   0

Contents

About This Book   **7**

The Good Samaritan   **11**

Giving Thanks   **17**

Love and Family   **23**

Friends   **29**

The Stranger   **37**

Islands of Honesty   **41**

Nice Guys Finish Last   **51**

Winning Isn't Everything   **55**

We Have Met the Enemy   **63**

Vengeance Is Mine   **69**

Spread It Around   **73**

Created Equal   **81**

But Not Forgotten **85**

Self-Respect **91**

Angels and Servants **97**

The Villain **103**

The Greatest Gift of All **107**

About This Book

"Whatever is true, whatever is honorable, whatever is just, whatever is pure, whatever is lovely, whatever is gracious, if there is any excellence, if there is anything worthy of praise, think about these things."

I doubt that many people have used the apostle Paul as their advertising agent, especially for a book about sports. But the above words, written in Philippians 4:8, describe perfectly what this book is about.

Even if you aren't one of us hopeless junkies who turns to the sports page of a newspaper before reading anything else, you're probably aware that sports news doesn't often carry the kinds of messages that Paul was talking about. The sports world is teeming with stories of violence and mayhem. Cocaine abuse and other drug problems infest the locker room. Bench-clearing brawls, tough talk, loud boasting, and ridicule of opponents all make good news copy. Scandals are brewing from one end of the country to the other as college booster clubs compete with numbers-running mobsters to see who can come up with the most creative methods of cheating. The dollar sign is practically stamped on the playing fields as we're bombarded with figures on who makes how much money, who's holding out for more, and how pro sports and even college sports are just businesses. The "virtues" that sports provide seem to have been swamped by the notion that, in order to survive in the sports world, you need more than talent and effort; you also need to be cocky, selfish, mean, and ruthless.

The purpose of this book is not to try and sweep all criticism of sports under a rug. Sports involve people and as such are subject to all manner of human failings, and it would be both negligent and irresponsible not to report the truth about them.

But there is another, quieter, side to sports. While researching sports books for the past eight years, I have been occasionally distracted from my task by stories of athletes whose clear vision of life helped them to see beyond the trophy case and the dotted line on a contract. Purely by accident, I found my thoughts pulled into the areas in which, according to Paul, we ought to spend more time. It seemed that these stories were some of the most valuable gifts that sport has to offer, and yet many of the stories were buried. Because of their heroic status in our world, athletes were being looked up to as role models and yet the best models, those that best displayed a Christian attitude toward life, were hidden away.

For the past few years, I've been digging for those stories—anything that was true and honorable, just and pure, anything gracious and touched by love, anything excellent and worthy of praise.

Just as God's gifts have been distributed among all kinds of people on the earth, so have these stories. I don't know the religious beliefs of all the people in this book. Some are outspoken Christian evangelists, some are quieter Christians, some may be members of faiths other than Christian, and some may not be a part of organized religion at all. But I believe that somehow the gifts from God that Paul was describing have passed through them to us. Christians not only can share in the wonder and beauty of these stories, but can learn a great deal from them about their faith, and about ways to follow the teachings and example of Jesus. For that purpose, complementary stories or verses from the Bible are suggested at the conclusion of each chapter.

An added benefit for me in this project was the generous help extended to me by many persons. Thank you to those contributors, with special appreciation and admiration for Josh Rosenfeld, Tracy Caulkins, Theresa Andrews, Wayne Minshew, Claude Mouton, and the Washington Redskins.

The Good Samaritan

Darryl Stingley broke out of the New England Patriots' huddle and trotted toward the right sideline. The Patriots had muscled their way down to the Oakland Raider 24-yard line, trying to squeeze in another score before half-time. It was third down and eight and Stingley knew that his team's chances of scoring might well depend on what he did in the next few seconds. Not that the world would crumble to ashes if he failed; after all, even though 53,000 people were watching him, this was only an exhibition game. Following his splendid 1977 season as New England's deep pass threat, Stingley had nothing to prove to the coaches. These exhibition games were just supposed to help him get ready for what he expected would be the best season of his career.

Over on the sideline, a beefy man who has often described himself as "that crazy coach who used to storm around the sidelines yelling at the officials" looked on. To outsiders, John Madden, coach of the Raiders, provided just one more reason to root against pro football's meanest, toughest team. The man's rantings and ravings with his shirt tails hanging out and his arms waving all over the air rubbed people the wrong way. After all, what did he have to complain about? In his nine years as field boss of the Raiders, Madden's men had won 94, lost only 25, and tied 7. New England was still smoldering over an unjust string of luck that had carried the Raiders past the Patriots in the 1976 play-offs and on to a Super Bowl win.

At the snap of the ball, Stingley sprinted downfield with Oakland's All-Pro defensive back, Mark Haynes, shadowing him. Suddenly he turned and streaked at a 45 degree angle toward the center of the field. Darryl Stingley had taken up the challenge of running the most dangerous pass pattern in football, one that would send him sprinting blindly into the sights of the safeties patrolling that area of the field.

Stingley knew that his pattern left him dangerously open to a brutal blind-side hit. But he also knew that he couldn't play football and not expect to get clobbered occasionally. He had taken tough hits before and shrugged them off, and so he dashed into no-man's land.

Out of the corner of his eye, Oakland safety Jack Tatum detected a fast-moving body invading his turf. Darryl Stingley wasn't going to get away with that. The 205-pound Tatum's reputation for torpedolike hits had stopped most other clubs from running that type of pattern against Oakland. Too many brash moves like Stingley's might tarnish that reputation. Ignoring the other Patriot receivers, Tatum prepared a greeting for Stingley that would make him think twice about running that kind of a pass pattern.

New England's young quarterback Steve Grogan didn't notice that his other wide receiver, Stanley Morgan, had broken free from his defender far downfield. Instead he waited for Stingley to pull away from Haynes. The timing of the pass had to be just right, and Grogan's throw wasn't even close. First he waited too long before throwing, and then he sailed the ball high over Stingley's head. Even for a receiver with the acrobatic talents of Stingley, there was no chance to make the catch, but the competitive instincts that helped him excel in the pros told him to try anyway.

As he stretched out after the ball, he saw an onrushing freight train wearing number 31 closing in on him. The computer in Stingley's mind calculated the force of the bone-crunching hit that the speeding 200-pound defender would deliver and instinctively Darryl ducked his head close to his body. But instead of cushioning the blow, it put Stingley's body, already vulnerable to a hard tackle, into the worst possible position. He took the brunt of the collision on his neck and fell to the ground, limp and unconscious. As Stingley was gingerly placed in an ambulance, the players knew he was hurt badly, but no one knew exactly how serious it was. Life went on, Stingley was replaced and the game completed.

The Patriots showered and dressed and shuffled off to the airplane that would take them back to New England, feeling badly for Darryl Stingley, who from the looks of it wouldn't be back in the lineup for a long time. Just as they were boarding the plane, an emergency phone call interrupted their departure. It was the Raider coach. After that third and eight play, football had been the last thing on John Madden's mind. He had followed up on Stingley's injury and found that Darryl's neck had been broken and that he would be lucky to survive the next few days. Quickly Madden had tracked down the Patriots to alert them before they left town.

When Stingley regained consciousness in the hospital,

the entire world seemed like a jigsaw puzzle in which none of the pieces fit. One of his first visions was that of the heavyset, blustery coach hovering over his bed. Confused and terrified, Stingley found that he couldn't move a muscle. Even the fingers on his hands wouldn't budge. With tears in his eyes, John Madden, the coach of New England's hated rival, sat next to the patient. Calmly the coach talked to him, held his hand, and gently touched his face. It was Madden who saw Stingley was having breathing problems and discovered that a suction machine that was needed to keep Darryl's breathing passages open had stopped functioning. The coach called for a nurse who was able to get the life-saving apparatus working again.

During the most intense days of final preparation for the new season, John Madden found time to visit Darryl at the hospital every day. He would talk easily and comfortably about football, about his team and their problems, and assure him that the Raiders were all pulling for him to recover quickly. Surrounded by strangers and racked by pain, Stingley looked forward to those visits. One day passed more slowly than usual for Darryl because it seemed that Madden had finally been overwhelmed by the demands of his job and had been unable to squeeze in a visit. But at a few minutes before midnight, the big coach walked through the hospital door. His team had flown to Denver to play a game that day. As soon as the plane landed back in Oakland, Madden had rushed out to the hospital to talk with Stingley.

When Stingley's family arrived in Oakland, Madden and his wife, Virginia, looked after them. Virginia had the family over for dinner and helped to get them settled in Oakland until Darryl could be moved back home.

John Madden resigned as coach of the Raiders at the end of the season, despite becoming only the second NFL head coach to win 100 games in his first 10 seasons. Since then he has gone on to become the most respected football broadcaster in the country. Stingley survived the nightmarish ordeal but the accident left him crippled for life. Sometimes, however, small lights shine most brightly in the blackest darkness. Had Darryl Stingley written down a list of the people he could really count on in crisis, the name of John Madden would never have been considered. There were so many good reasons why Madden shouldn't have gotten so involved. It wasn't his player; he didn't even know the man. But in reflecting on those first awful days, Stingley said that the only people he trusted were his own family and John Madden. In the midst of tragedy Stingley was able to see what even Madden's most devoted fans might not have known. That the game of football wasn't nearly as important to John Madden as the human beings who played it.

Read Luke 10:25-37 for the story of another person who went far out of his way to get involved in another man's problems, the original good Samaritan.

Giving Thanks

If Mike Bossy had it to do over again he might have played dumb, as if he didn't know or care about the hallowed record he was threatening. But he had come right out and announced to the whole world that he was gunning for Maurice "Rocket" Richard's National Hockey League (NHL) scoring mark. Now Bossy could blame no one but himself for the awkward spot he was in, and for the maddening barrage of questions as a pack of reporters stuck with him like a bad case of dandruff.

"Well, Mike, can you still do it? What do you think your chances are of breaking The Rocket's record? How does it feel to be so close? Do you think that you're starting to press too much? Are you sleeping at night?" Mike had called in the spotlights, but now the heat from those lights had started to blister his peace of mind.

During the 1944–1945 season, Rocket Richard, the pride of the hockey powerhouse known as the Montreal Canadiens, had taken off on an incredible scoring binge. Careening around the ice with the furious abandon of a charioteer, Richard had scored a record 50 goals during the 50-game season. Since that time, the NHL schedule had been expanded to 80 games, which padded scoring totals to the point where nearly every team in the league boasted a 50-goal scorer. "Fifty goals in a season?" snorted the experts. "Doesn't mean a thing anymore. If Richard were given that many chances he'd wear out the nets! Let someone score 50 goals in 50 games like he did and then we can start making comparisons to The Rocket." For 36 years no one had been able to meet the challenge, and now Mike Bossy suggested that he was going to do it.

No one had to prime Bossy's pump about the 50/50 record. For him, Rocket Richard was more than just a name out of the past. Mike had been born in Montreal in 1957, when Richard and the Flying Canadiens practically owned the city. Like thousands of Canadian boys, Bossy had believed that learning to walk was just a preliminary to the really important business of learning how to skate. Unlike the others, however, Mike quickly showed that he shared Richard's ability to put a puck in the net.

The art of consistent goal-scoring has always been somewhat of a mystery, but in Bossy's case it seemed almost a miscarriage of justice. His shot wasn't powerful enough to sting anyone and he couldn't skate all that swiftly. He hadn't the size or the muscle to bounce bodies around the ice as Richard did, nor could he plant himself in front of the net to collect garbage goals off rebounds. Nevertheless, the gentle New York Islander racked up some very Richard-like scoring numbers, including a league-leading 69 goals in 1978–1979. Somehow Bossy was usually in the right spot at the right time and his shot seemed to be magnetically attracted to the back of the net. Opponents swore that when Bossy shot a puck it could alter its flight in midair to avoid a goalie.

Bossy wasn't content with leading the league, though. In the back of his mind he reserved a spot for himself alongside his hometown hero in the 50/50 club. When Mike drilled 40 goals in his first 41 games of the 1980–1981 season, he could contain his ambition no longer. Once he opened his mouth to issue the challenge, Bossy was a marked man. While reporters dogged him off the ice, opposing defensemen practically climbed inside his jersey. Some teams seemed to care less about beating the Islanders than they did about keeping Bossy out of the record books.

Bossy's glorious march to immortality turned into a nightmare. After coming so close, with 48 goals in 47 games, his hopes plummeted as he was handcuffed in his next two games. Worse yet, he had to stew while Los Angeles' Charlie Simmer, who had made no boasts about Richard's 50/50 mark, nearly stole his thunder. Simmer's goal-scoring flurry drew him to within an ice shaving of the mark as he tallied 49 goals in 50 games.

A harried Mike Bossy skated onto the ice for his game number 50 with only a flickering hope. If he couldn't break out of his slump and score two goals that evening against the Quebec Nordiques, Richard's record would survive yet another year.

For two periods Bossy played with all the grace and confidence of a camel on ice. Later he said that it felt as though his hands were stuck together. Skating with mo-lasses-tipped blades, he generally reached a loose puck just as a Quebec player poke-checked it away. Bossy's coach and teammates knew what the record meant to Bossy and they did their best to help him out. Coach Al Arbour kept his ace out on the ice for extra long shifts, and the Islander players dug feverishly in the corners to free the puck, trying to set up a good shot for Bossy. Despite their best efforts, though, New York's star scorer could not manage so much as one weak shot on goal.

With only 20 minutes remaining in the game, Bossy had to face the facts. Not only was his dream rapidly slipping away, he was humiliating himself with his feeble effort. After boldly defying the pressure of chasing records, he was now wilting under that pressure like a rose in a vegetable steamer. Bossy decided to quit focusing on the dream; he had to shake off the nerves, play as hard as he could and let the scoring take care of itself.

For the first 14 minutes of the final period, Bossy worked harder and played better. It still didn't help him score, but at least he couldn't fault his effort. With six minutes left in the game, which was tied 4–4, Quebec was caught committing a penalty, that gave the Islanders a one-man advantage for two minutes. Realistically, Bossy had to score on this power play or the 50/50 record chase would be over. The New York players whipped sharp passes around the Nordique defense. Suddenly Bossy lashed a shot on goal that sped past the Quebec goalie. Goal number 49 was in the bag! He still had a chance.

Fewer than two minutes remained when Bossy jumped over the boards after a brief rest. His linemate and best friend, Bryan Trottier, charged into the Nordique end and fought his way through a maze of defenders. Although not quite the scorer that Bossy was, many experts considered Trottier the better all-around player. Without Trottier's gritty determination in digging the puck out of corners and crowds and his clever passes, Bossy would have been like a rifle without ammunition. As Trottier moved in on the goal, out of the corner of his eye he spotted Bossy weaving into scoring position. Bossy wasn't sure that Trottier could see him. But when the pass arrived he was ready. No sooner had the puck touched his stick than Mike flicked it into the open corner of the net.

His arms shot high in the air in celebration and he soaked up the sensations of a dream come true: the echoing shouts, the flashing red lights, and gloved fists pounding his back! The suffocating blanket of pressure dissolved as from the brink of despair Bossy found himself standing on a peak that only Rocket Richard had been able to scale: 50 goals in 50 games!

But Bossy had barely finished peeling his happy teammates off him when an even greater opportunity opened up. With time running out on them in the game, the trailing Nordiques attacked the Islander net so furiously that they were caught on the wrong end of the ice when Bossy gathered in a loose puck. Only one Nordique defenseman was scrambling back to bar Mike's path to the goal, and that defenseman had to keep one eye on Bryan Trottier, who was streaking up the ice with Bossy. Mike zeroed in on the goal, preparing for the shot that could make him the best goal-scorer of all time.

What happened as Bossy crossed the blue line into the attacking zone could not have been planned. In that blur of action there could not have been time for him to ponder the contributions that Trottier had made to his scoring mark. There could not have been time to remember the days when Bossy had been a scared rookie, overwhelmed by the intimidating vastness and bustle of New York City, when Trottier had taken him into his home and helped settle his fears. Nor could his memory have played back the companionship of their many nights as drinking buddies, downing their milkshakes and enduring the ribbing of their more hard-living teammates.

But as he drew his stick back for that shot of a lifetime, the intoxication of success suddenly blew away. Mike Bossy remembered to give thanks.

The sports world has developed a number of sportsmanlike ways for the prime-time players to give credit to their mates. They can modestly mention in interviews the importance of teamwork. After ramming an easy dunk shot through the net, a pro basketball player will often point to the person whose pass allowed him to slam dunk. Great running backs take their blockers out to dinner and give them watches.

Somehow an after-the-fact tribute wasn't enough to cover what Bossy felt. In a split second of debate, he found a better way to say thank you. Rather than reaching out for more glory, Mike Bossy fed the puck to a startled Trottier, who rammed it past an even more startled goalie for the score. History may have been robbed that night but Bossy showed no regrets. "After all he's done for me, I owed him that one," he said.

Read Luke 17:11-19 for the story of a man who, while others got so caught up in wild excitement and triumph, remembered to give thanks to the one who made it all possible.

Love and Family

For those forecasters who liked to play their sports on paper weeks before the actual event, the women's 100-meter backstroke in the 1984 Olympics posed a stiff challenge. Some predicted victory for the East Germans, others favored the Romanians. United States record holder Sue Walsh couldn't be overlooked either, nor could her teammate Betsy Mitchell. Behind these front-runners swam a vast flotilla of loyal troopers who would struggle gamely but would end up gasping in the froth kicked up by these faster swimmers. Slotted for this group was a young woman named Theresa Andrews. What the experts didn't realize, however, was that Andrews had the others outnumbered. Invisible to outsiders, Danny Andrews was in the water helping with every stroke and kick.

Only one year before the Olympics, Theresa had been immersed in what might have been the highlight of her 14-year swimming career. She had made the United States team for the Pan American Games and was preparing for her race when she received a phone call. Her 20-year-old brother Danny had been in an accident, no details.

As the 9th and 10th children of a tightly knit family of 12 kids, Theresa and Danny had been especially close. When Theresa returned home she found that her brother, an All-American lacrosse player, had been permanently crippled when struck by a car. Devastated, she took a year off from her classes at the University of Florida to help Danny with his rehabilitation. Some might have considered it a sacrifice, but it soon became obvious that Theresa Andrews had merely signed up to train with the best coach in the land.

Immediately Theresa could tell that Danny was in no danger of being defeated by the injury. Nurses told her that the first thing he had asked after learning of his disability was "How's everyone else taking it?" Trying to understand what Danny was going through, Theresa probed him for details of what it felt like to be paralyzed. "I could sit around and feel bad," he answered. "But I want to be a happy person so I look for the good things."

That attitude rubbed off as the two went into training together. When Theresa's legs begged her for rest, she would be thankful that those legs could still bend and kick, and she continued to work. When she was most tired during a running workout she made up her mind to tack an extra half mile onto the run. After each workout, the two Andrews would talk over how well or how badly things were going.

Even with this inspiration, Theresa began to feel the walls closing in on her. Doomsday approached—the Olympic trials. Fourteen years of effort was coming down to its final judgment. To make matters worse, the Olympic rules had been toughened. Only two swimmers from each country would be allowed to compete in the 1984 Olympics instead of the three that had been allowed in previous years. With Walsh and Mitchell swimming well, Andrews had to face the grim probability that she wouldn't make the team.

The threat of failure finally broke down Theresa Andrews. Not for a moment in all her years of training had she given a thought of quitting. But in December of 1983 she just sat around the house, refusing to work out any more. Again it was Danny to the rescue. "Don't worry about us," he said. "If you don't make the team it's no bad reflection on you or the rest of us. You've come this far; just do the best that you can."

Focusing on Danny's positive spirit, Andrews was able to put workouts back into perspective. The Olympic Games were not the secret to the meaning of life. Ending her two-week retirement, Theresa dedicated herself to Danny's philosophy of looking for the best. Suddenly those nagging worries that had been twisting her into knots seemed to let go. Instead of fretting about being a couple of pounds heavy or a second too slow, she perked herself up by dwelling on the things she was doing well. The more she improved, the more she could feel Danny's excitement in her progress, and that made the work seem easier.

The two-qualifiers-per-event rule turned the United States Olympic Trials into a brutal contest of survival. More than 200 swimmers posted times fast enough to qualify for the Olympics, but only 43 of those made the team. One of those 43 was a surprisingly cool Theresa Andrews. She edged out Sue Walsh to claim the second spot in the 100 meters behind Betsy Mitchell.

At the 1984 Olympics in Los Angeles, Andrews swam in the shadow of such intimidating opponents as six-foot, three-inch Carmen Bunaciu of Romania. But after swimming her best race ever in the preliminaries, Theresa found herself nudging closer to the spotlight. The race had felt so easy and yet only one swimmer in the entire field had beaten her time. As she studied the results her first thought was, "If I could get a medal I could give it to Danny."

With an Olympic medal suddenly a very real possibility, the electricity surged through her nervous system. Feeling like a skittish horse in a room full of rattlesnakes, she waited by the pool as time slowed to a crawl. When she heard her name announced, for the final race she turned to the stands on her left searching for a familiar face. There was Danny wearing a grin so huge that it melted away her nervousness.

Theresa swam loosely and confidently and when she touched the wall at the finish line she knew she had done well. Unable to see the scoreboard, however, she didn't know how well. It wasn't until her teammate, Betsy Mitchell, congratulated her 30 seconds later that she realized she had won. The Romanians had fallen back, and Andrews had touched home less than a tenth of a second before Mitchell.

Four other United States swimmers won golds that day, and one way or another, they grabbed the headlines away from Andrews. News reports highlighted the furor over a controversial start in one of the races, and commentaries zeroed in on the questionable sportsmanship of another swimmer who expressed disgust with himself after winning his gold. But behind the scenes, Theresa Andrews, who also took a gold medal in the 400-meter medley relay, completed a more memorable story by presenting Danny Andrews with his medal. "After all, he had an Olympic year," she said.

Read Ruth 1:11-18 for the story of a woman who stayed with a family member in hard times and whose positive attitude boosted the spirits of her mother-in-law.

Friends

1

If it had happened on a tradition-rich team such as the Boston Celtics instead of getting lost in the nomadic wanderings of the Sacramento-Kansas City-Omaha-Cincinnati-Rochester Kings-Royals, the rays of friendship that surrounded Maurice Stokes might still be lighting up the corners of the NBA courts.

Maurice Stokes was built like a football player but he could do more things with a basketball than any center of his time. In three years with the Rochester-Cincinnati Royals, he averaged more than 16 points per game, led the league in rebounds, and, incredibly for a center, ranked as high as third in assists. Unfortunately, other than the soft-shooting forward Jack Twyman, the Royals' talent pool ran dust dry. So it was a proud accomplishment when in 1957, Stokes led the Royals to the playoffs for the first time in his three-year career.

The team's 100–83 loss to Detroit in their first play-off game chipped some of the finish off that pride, however. After a sluggish, 12-point, 15-rebound effort, Stokes welcomed the chance to fly back to Cincinnati to regroup for the next game. Suddenly it seemed as though a flu bug went screaming through his body. The big man tried to tough out the flight home but after repeated vomiting, fever, and chills, he fell into a coma. Flight attendants radioed ahead for an ambulance and Stokes was both baptized and given last rites on the plane. Only with ice packs, a tracheotomy, feeding tubes, and other emergency hospital measures was the Royals' star kept alive.

At first doctors thought the 24-year-old had come down with sleeping sickness. But a check of Cincinnati's games revealed that he had been knocked off balance going up for a rebound in a recent contest and had slammed his head on the floor. Although he had seemed alright at the time, Maurice Stokes had suffered a serious brain injury.

Without their star, the Royals quickly bowed out of the playoffs and scattered to their homes across the country. Jack Twyman, however, lived in Cincinnati and visited Stokes frequently as the big man struggled for four months to pull out of his coma. When Stokes did awake, it was "like being buried alive." He was totally paralyzed and could not even talk.

For awhile Twyman was rocked by that helpless feeling that gnaws at us when we're exposed to someone else's tragedy. But suddenly it became clear to him that there were some real problems that he could do something about. Stokes's family had quietly despaired of finding the money to continue Maurice's care. Maurice had lived by himself and no one knew what he had done with his money. "Don't worry about the money or the bills," Twyman told the family. "I'll see that it's taken care of."

With painstaking thoroughness, Twyman searched all the Cincinnati banks until he found Stokes's accounts. Despite having a family with small children to care for,

Twyman had himself appointed legal guardian so that he could supervise Stokes's affairs and pay all the bills.

Extensive hospital care was expensive, though, and Twyman turned his energy to other sources. His moving appeal to the NBA board of governors resulted in the scheduling of a couple of exhibition games to raise money for the ex-Royal. The Royals, Hawks, Celtics, and Pistons paid their own expenses to put on the charity double-header. In an era before charity fund-raising techniques were polished, Twyman generated enough publicity so that many fans sent contributions to the cause. Even small children cracked into their banks and sent what pennies they could afford. Twyman tried everything he could think of to raise money, from selling donated grocery items to arranging a concert.

Not content with the impersonal, behind the scenes work, Twyman worked hard to help his friend to relearn such basic skills as chewing and swallowing. Seven months after the accident, Twyman devised a way for Stokes to break out of the bubble of silence that trapped him. Time after time, Jack would recite the alphabet, and when he reached the letter that Maurice wanted, Stokes would blink. In this agonizingly slow method, Stokes could spell out what he wanted to say. When Maurice finally regained a flicker of movement in his fingers, Twyman drew a typewriter keyboard on some cardboard so that his friend could spell out what he wanted.

The best part of it all was that the seemingly enormous burden of help that Twyman had taken upon himself did not drag him down at all. Many times Jack insisted that he was getting far more out of working with Maurice

31

than the "patient" was. Having Maurice as a new "member of the family" certainly had no ill effect on Twyman's pro career. In 1960 he quietly averaged 31.2 points per game. Had Wilt Chamberlain not been in the league that year, Twyman's mark would have made him the top single season scorer in NBA history. The Cincinnati cornerman finished his career with more than 15,000 points. Yet nothing he did on the court could have touched the hearts of basketball fans as did one letter inspired by Jack Twyman's special friendship with Maurice Stokes. Along with a cash contribution came the oft-quoted words, "Where else but in this country could I, a Jew, send money to you, a Catholic, to help a black man?"

2

The sweat had been spilled, the pain conquered, and now it was time to step out of the grimy uniform, sit back and enjoy the rewards. One of these rewards was about to be placed in the palms of Gale Sayers, the Chicago Bears' great running back. Ever since he had broken into the NFL with 22 touchdowns in 1965, Sayers had heard himself described as the most exciting open-field runner in NFL history. In 1968, however, his career seemed to have been snapped along with the ligaments in his knee following a wrenching tackle at the hands of the San Francisco 49ers. Sayers had come back from this terrible injury, though, to lead the league in rushing in 1969. Now an expensively dressed audience in New York at the Pro Football Writers' dinner was applauding him as he strode to the microphone to accept the George S. Halas Award as the NFL's most courageous player during the 1969 season.

It should have been a proud moment for Sayers but his thoughts were not on his own comeback efforts. Instead he kept seeing the face of a man he called "Pick."

Brian Piccollo had joined the Bears the same year that Sayers had. Despite having led the nation in rushing at Wake Forest University, Piccollo's lack of size and speed labeled him as just another body cluttering up the practice field. But, as Sayers now knew better than anyone else, Pick was something different. What other white kid from the south would joke, upon being assigned a locker between Dick Gordon and Gale Sayers, both black, that "I feel like an Oreo cookie"? Who else would treat the magnificent Mr. Sayers as just another working stiff?

It was in 1967 that the Bears decided it was time to stop segregating players by color on road trips and had approached Sayers to make the first move. The man Sayers had chosen had been that tough, rascally, hardworking back who was still on the team two years after many had expected him to be cut, and who had been needling Sayers the entire time. Piccollo hadn't been exactly thrilled about his new roomie, but went along with it good-naturedly, quipping there would be no problem as long as Gale didn't try to use the bathroom.

For awhile the two did little more than put in time together in their shared cubicle but gradually they grew to like each other. When Sayers had been wracked with doubts following his knee injury, Piccollo had kept after him, alternately encouraging him about his progress and chiding him for being too timid in testing it.

Life's wrinkles finally seemed to be ironing themselves out for the roomies in 1969. Sayers had worked his knee back into fighting shape and Piccollo had worked himself into more playing time in the backfield. Then Piccollo had begun to cough. First thing in the morning, he would start hacking, and then later at night more fits of coughing. Normally it took a court injunction to force Piccollo off the practice field, but suddenly he couldn't go the distance at Bear workouts.

A check with the doctors revealed why. Brian Piccollo, who had checked out perfectly healthy a couple of months ago, was in the death grip of a grapefruit-sized tumor eating into his lungs. They operated in November of 1969, hoping to remove it all. Sayers and some of his teammates quickly volunteered to give blood and Piccollo with his unbeatable spirit joked that after the transfusion he suddenly had a strange hankering for fried chicken. Visits to the patient's room were never somber or gloomy or awkward. Piccollo's cheerful bantering and light insults kept the air clear from being saturated with pity. While in grave danger of dying himself, Brian Piccollo managed to sneak away to a different room to visit a small girl who had only a few weeks to live following a broken neck.

This Pro Football Writers' dinner hadn't gone the way Sayers had hoped. His plan had been to get Piccollo to come with him to the awards dinner, but Brian had been too sick. So now as the applause died down, the great Bears' star graciously accepted the award and then stunned the crowd into electric silence by telling them that they had given it to the wrong person. He told them that the amount of courage he had shown was not much more than a bluff compared to the 24-hour-a-day courage of a little-known reserve running back. "This award is mine tonight, but it's Brian Piccollo's tomorrow," he said. "I love Brian Piccollo. Tonight, ask God to love him, too."

Brian Piccollo died a few months later.

Read Matthew 22:37-39 and 1 John 3:17-18 for words that inspire people to act as Twyman and Sayers did.

The Stranger

Maybe Bart Starr's neck wasn't exactly on the chopping block, but if he listened carefully he could hear the whine of the grindstone sharpening the executioner's blade. The ex-quarterback owed his survival as the Green Bay Packer coach to the long memories of Packer fans who still admired him for his role as leader of the Pack in their glory years of the 1960s. But after eight years of struggling to bring those glory days back to Green Bay, Starr was running out of time.

A 5–3–1 record and a play-off berth in the strike-shortened 1982 season had bought another year for Starr. But even that success paled when compared with the glory days, the standard by which Packer fans measured their teams. A winning record was only a start; the Packers had to keep getting better.

As he brought his team into New York for a Monday night game against the Giants, Starr was confident that his team was ready. Green Bay had posted two victories in their first three games of 1983. Quarterback Lynn Dickey, free of nagging injuries, finally had the pass protection he needed to riddle enemy defenses. Going into the Giant game, the Pack Attack had struck for a fraction under 30 points per game. Although the defense still offered only a fair imitation of the stingy Packer defenses of yesterday, they could keep the Giants well under control. After all, New York had totaled only 35 points in their three games, two of which were losses.

The fact that the game was on national television pushed the stakes higher. The stage was set for Starr to broadcast the unmistakable message to the country that "the Pack was back."

Something went wrong. It was like showing up at a dinner in your honor and discovering you'd forgotten to put on your pants. As Starr and Packer fans across the nation looked on in horror, the Green Bay team bumbled and staggered their way to a humiliating defeat. There was a halfhearted effort by the tight end who seemed to have a clear path to the goal line only to be pulled down in the open field by a much smaller defender. The kickoff returner fumbled the ball into Giant hands not once but twice. Turning the game into a slapstick comedy, Green Bay coughed up the ball again when one of their men blocking for a punt returner let the ball hit him in the back of the leg.

New York's anemic running game barreled over, around, and through the Packer defense for 208 yards. Meanwhile Green Bay's blocking wall turned to cardboard. Lynn Dickey was sacked three times and harassed most of the night, while the runners gained only 53 yards in 21 tries. Even the television broadcasters threw away all charity and described the contest as ridiculous, inept, and a disaster. Instead of marching proudly off the field as established contenders, the Packers had to slink off the field on the low side of a 27–3 score.

No one could have been more crushed than Bart Starr.

He had once been the symbol of flawless football crafts-manship. The Packer offense had made fewer mistakes than a top surgeon during the glory days while he was taking the snaps from center. Now he was reduced to a below average coach, whose record in pros was a hum-bling 47-71-3, whose team had played so badly that the network sponsors were covering their eyes in embar-rassment. As the head coach, he had to stand up in the front of the room and take responsibility for the disaster. It was he who had to face reporters, field their harsh questions, and admit that "we embarrassed ourselves." The confidence and consistency that had eluded his team for eight years had finally seemed within reach only to be blown away again by a mocking wind. It would be a long flight home as he tried to pick up the pieces of the gut-wrenching defeat, to search yet again for answers as to what went wrong.

The flight turned out to be longer than he had ex-pected. As if the heavens themselves were in on the conspiracy to destroy Bart Starr, a thick fog rolled in over Green Bay. With the Green Bay airport socked in by fog much of the night, the plane carrying the weary, de-moralized Packers couldn't land there until 3:00 A.M.

In the wee hours of Tuesday morning, Emery Coonen was feeling every bit as exhausted as the Packers. He had just finished his 12-hour work shift at the Fort How-ard Paper Company in Green Bay and was driving home in the damp darkness. The guardian angels had totally deserted the city of Green Bay that night, and Emery Coonen was not going to escape either. As he pulled onto the Allouez-Ashwaubenon bridge, his pick-up truck sputtered and choked itself to a stop. There wasn't much traffic at that hour of the night, and it is not a time that inspires motorists to acts of trust or charity. Coonen could hardly have picked a worse time to run out of gas.

A number of bright headlights rolled into view and Coonen signaled for help. No one even slowed down. Home seemed impossibly far away until one automobile carrying a man and a woman finally slowed down. The flicker of hope was quickly squelched, however, as the car drove off, leaving Coonen alone and frustrated.

Ten minutes later, however, the same car returned, this time with only one passenger. After driving his wife home, the man had come back to see what Coonen needed. Within a short time the stranger had located some gasoline, and brought it back. At last Emery Coonen could get himself home for a well-deserved rest. Before driving off, he asked the stranger what he owed him for his time and for the gas. The stranger refused to accept anything but thanks, saying, "It might be me who needs help next time."

At that the stranger left and drove back to his home. On a night when he had every right to circle his wagons against the world and anguish about the overwhelming rash of bad luck that had befallen him, Bart Starr had instead reached out in an act of kindness to a total stranger.

Read Matthew 25:35-40 to find out why it was so important for Bart Starr to lend a helping hand on the road that night.

Islands of Honesty

Television announcers review an isolated replay that shows an offensive lineman grabbing and tackling a defensive lineman. "Hey, there's nothing wrong with that as long as you can get away with it," they chuckle. A hockey coach subtly tosses some pennies on the ice. Officials have to call a time out to clean up the mess, which gives the coach's panting players some valuable moments of rest. College officials excuse recruiting violations by saying that they have to cheat in order to be competitive with all the other cheaters. A comedian gets his audience howling at the absurdity of his story of a catcher who admits to an umpire that the runner really did beat his tag.

If it's true that sports build character, why do they give the virtue of honesty such a beating? Perhaps it is because sports do not build character, they merely test it. Meet three men who passed this most difficult test with honors.

1

Bobby Jones refused to take golf too seriously. It was a game, a hobby, a challenging way to use his leisure time. Jones certainly wasn't interested in making a living at it. The law was his profession and means of earning money; golf was just an enjoyable way to spend it. It wasn't an obsession with him, either. He didn't spend his waking moments plotting his strategy for the next 18 holes. If he could find time for a few rounds of golf during eight months of the year, he was content to find something else to do the other four months.

If he happened to win a tournament along the way, well, that was a nice bonus. As it turned out, Bobby Jones won more than a few tournaments, and these weren't just friendly bets for quarters and free golf balls at the local club. During his career, Jones entered 52 major golf tournaments and won 23 of them! He retired from the sport at 28, an age when many top golfers are still honing their skills. Some consider him the greatest golfer of all time, and speculate as to how many tournaments he would have won had he even taken up the game full time. Included in his triumphs were four United States Open titles, five U.S. Amateur championships, and three wins in the British Open.

Perhaps his greatest victory, however, came in the 1925 United States Open held at the Worcester Country Club in Massachusetts. Playing against the top professionals in the world, Jones found himself in the thick of a battle royal for first place. Gene Sarazen, Walter Hagen, Willie MacFarlane, and four others were all bobbing for the lead in the two-day, 72-hole tournament.

Bobby Jones started slowly with a first round score of 77 that dropped him into the middle of the pack. His second round 70, however, catapulted him to 10th place, and a repeat of that score on round three had him breathing down the necks of the leaders.

During one of the rounds, Jones found a hole that stubbornly resisted taming. It was on the 11th tee that he uncharacteristically whacked his ball out of the carefully groomed fairway and found it perched in a precarious position on a hill in the rough grass. After selecting his club, Jones took his stance over the ball and peered down the course to where the flag was. Looking back at the ball, Jones suddenly shocked onlookers by declaring a penalty on himself! Both spectators and playing partners stared at each other dumbfounded. What was Jones talking about?

According to tournament rules, if your ball moves while you are addressing it (that is, standing over it preparing to swing), a one-shot penalty must be assessed. Jones had seen what no other pair of eyes on the face of the earth could have seen, that his ball had shifted the distance of just a couple of grass blades. No one really thought Jones should take a penalty for that, but Bobby insisted that the rule be followed.

The eight contenders charged neck-and-neck toward the final hole, and one by one they stumbled on the threshold of victory. When the last shot had been drained into the cup, first place was still up for grabs. Bobby Jones and Willie MacFarlane had finished in a dead tie. Like a pair of evenly matched arm wrestlers locked in their grip, neither budging, Jones and MacFarlane dueled for 18 extra holes without breaking their tie. Another 18-hole play-off was called for, and this time MacFarlane scrambled back from a four-stroke deficit to eek out a one-stroke victory. If it weren't for the unseen penalty he had called on himself, Bobby Jones would have won his fifth U.S. Open championship. But for Jones, the question of which he would rather carry around with him for the rest of his life, a golf championship or his integrity, was no contest.

2

In June of 1943 the New York Yankees, looking for their third straight major league championship, found the Washington Senators swaggering into their path. The Senators, only three games back in the standings, entered Yankee Stadium with talk about ending another in a series of Yankee dynasties.

Through five innings, the Yankees easily held off the upstarts, leading 1–0. New York's rookie pitcher, Butch Wensloff, had been sailing easily through the Senator lineup when he suddenly ran aground in the sixth. With two strokes of the bat, a single and a home run put Washington into the lead. Normally the young Yankee pitcher had little trouble finding home plate with his pitches, but under pressure, his compass suddenly went haywire. The next two batters walked, bringing up Washington's third baseman, Ellis Clary.

Clary was Wensloff's best hope of escape from the tight spot he'd wedged himself into. A part-time utility player known more for his glove than his bat, Clary probably couldn't hit Wensloff's worst pitch as far as the outfield bleachers. No need to be cautious, just throw strikes. Wensloff, however, still hadn't found his control. Clary didn't move the bat off his shoulder as the first two pitches went for balls. Wensloff tried again. This time he'd come close but the umpire ruled that the pitch was inside for ball three.

That was more than the frustrated Wensloff could take.

Insisting that the pitch was a strike, he began to argue with the umpire. New York manager Joe McCarthy flew to his pitcher's defense, berating the umpire for his lack of judgment and vision.

Looking on calmly at the dust storm his manager was raising was catcher Bill Dickey. Long considered the prime example of Yankee "class," Gentleman Bill was now finishing off his long career, biding his time while the baseball Hall of Fame cleared away a spot for him. Dickey's power had evaporated in this, his last productive year of ball. The aging hinges in his knees could no longer take that daily bending behind the plate. But when given enough chance to rest he could still hit for average and win games with his glove.

McCarthy's protests were growing louder and angrier when he turned to his catcher for support. It never hurt to have such a respected citizen as the great Bill Dickey backing up your argument. "Was it a strike?" he demanded.

"No," said Dickey. It was as if a plug had been pulled on a movie projector in the middle of a ferocious battle scene. Without another word, McCarthy returned sheepishly to the dugout. He should have known better. You asked Bill Dickey a question, he'd tell you the truth. New York went on to blow away the Senators by 13½ games to win their third straight pennant.

3

When Jim Wacker arrived to coach the football team at Texas Christian University in 1983, he didn't promise to be normal, or serious, or predictable. The one thing he did promise was that Texas Christian was going to run the cleanest football program in the country. Never mind that many of the teams in his conference were under investigation for recruiting violations and illegal cash payments to athletes. TCU was going to show them that you didn't have to cheat to win.

Up to that time, cheering for the Horned Frogs of TCU was a little like cheering for a pane of glass to break the rock that was thrown at it. For 25 years TCU hadn't been able to win, cheating or no cheating. In his first year Wacker seemed right at home with the tradition as his team posted a 1–8–2 record.

But within a year, Wacker had inspired a large part of north Texas to start rooting for the underfrog. His crazy television show, during which he once showed a highlight film clip of himself falling flat on his face, became a hit in Dallas. Astoundingly, the lowly Horned Frogs suddenly jumped all over their opponents, gang-tackling their way to an 8-4 record in 1984 and their first postseason bowl appearance in 19 years.

Best of all, this six-foot, five-inch son of a Detroit minister had done it the honest way, just as he had in building powerhouse squads at Texas Lutheran and Southwest Texas State. When a coach interviewing for a job on his staff boasted of his expertise in arranging deals to recruit star athletes, Wacker said he wasn't interested. Wacker extracted promises from powerful alumni boosters that no one was paying off TCU players. He urged rival coaches to join him in cleaning up the cheating in college recruiting, a move that received a cool response.

After winning Coach of the Year honors for pumping life into the TCU football program, Wacker looked forward to the 1985 season. The Horned Frogs were still on a roll, blasting Tulane by a score of 30–13 in their first game. Meanwhile, the conference was being swamped with rumors of illegal payoffs and recruiting violations, and even TCU's name got dragged into the mud. Coach Wacker welcomed anyone to look under all the carpets and into all the closets of the TCU program. On Thursday evening, September 19, he held a meeting to tell his team how proud he was of them for building a winning program without any under-the-table deals.

The speech may have swelled the chests of most of the Horned Frogs but it pricked the consciences of a few others. As a matter of fact, some of the players were being secretly bankrolled by alumni. All-American running back Keith Davis, for example had been promised thousands of dollars by TCU recruiters before Wacker arrived. Some of the players came forward immediately to tell Wacker that they were receiving illegal payments, others confided to assistant coaches.

Wacker was devastated. His honest program, that he had held up as a shining example of dedication and high principle turned out to be riddled with corruption. The deals were so carefully hidden that they probably would never have been found out, and they certainly weren't Wacker's fault; it had all happened before he arrived. Under more damaging circumstances, many other schools had protested their innocence, covered up the facts, or tried legal maneuvers to keep from hurting their money-making sports programs. That wasn't Jim Wacker's way, though.

After wringing the truth from some alumni backers, the TCU coach immediately notified the conference, and the National Collegiate Athletic Association. Although it was the hardest thing he'd ever been forced to do in his career, he also suspended the seven players who had received illegal payments.

TCU scraped past lowly Kansas State that Saturday, 24–22. But the rest of the season was a disastrous return to business as usual for the Horned Frogs. Wacker's highly-rated team was stampeded out of the stadium by SMU, and suffered humiliating shutouts at the hands of Arkansas and Baylor. They lost all eight conference matches, and ended up with a 3–8 overall mark.

Worse yet, the NCAA examined the evidence that Wacker had handed to them and rang down a brutal judgment upon TCU. The Horned Frogs were banned from bowl games during the 1986 season, were forced to pay back $300,000 in television income, and were stripped of 35 football scholarships over the next two years.

The players, who felt victimized by the whole system, didn't back Wacker's actions 100%. Many people called his actions foolish. Others told him he was a hero for taking a stand for honesty when so many others were winking at violations and hemming and hawing about the need for a crackdown on cheats. Wacker didn't feel like a hero, especially after the harsh punishment the NCAA had issued despite his cooperation. When asked why he did it, he responded, "Because Wacker's an idiot."

Jim Wacker's commitment to an honest program was so great that he was willing to back it up with a blank check. Eventually he was asked to pay a steep price to keep his program honest. Even though he may have been overcharged, Wacker honored the check.

What did Jones, Dickey, and Wacker gain from telling

the truth when it would have been to their advantage not to? Read Psalm 15 for one answer.

Nice Guys Finish Last

"But everyone does it" is not just an excuse that children use. Grownups have been known to resort to that time-honored sandbag to hold back the tide of conscience whenever it starts to spill over onto their questionable actions. Nowhere is this more obvious than in pro basketball, which was originally intended as, and is still naively labeled, a non-contact sport.

In May of 1986, pro basketball's last link with the rules was severed when Bobby Jones of the Philadelphia 76ers played the final game of his 12-year career. An NBA coach once said, "Watching Bobby Jones on a basketball court is like watching an honest man in a liars' poker game." Even the most respected of his coaches has had to wrestle with the problem, Is Bobby Jones too nice to do the job in a rough game? They knew he could be more effective if he used the tricks that all the other players used, and yet who could bring himself to demand that he abandon the Christian principles that made him the most admired player in the game? Bobby Jones never budged an inch on his principles and yet, working at an enormous disadvantage created by his own lofty values, he played at an All-Star level for many years.

"Let's play good, tough defense out there!" yells the coach. One player leans on his opponent, bangs him with his hip, and bodies him away from the basket. Out on the point, a guard drapes himself around his opponent, with a hand on the man's waist to "feel" which direction he's going. Other players cutting toward the basket are held, hooked, clawed, tripped, and elbowed—all with swift, subtle movements nearly undetectable by the human eye. A lightning jab or forearm knocks an opponent off balance, a push with the leg keeps him away from a rebound. At the slightest contact, the defender flies backward as if hit by an exploding grenade as he draws a charging foul.

It's all good, tough defense and it's very effective. The only problem is that all those moves are illegal. Referees don't whistle fouls for such offenses often because if they did, pro basketball would turn into a dull free-throw shooting contest. Tough defense has become an accepted part of the game.

When Robert Clyde Jones was taught those techniques, however, he said, "When I have to play defense by holding on, that's when I quit playing."

You never saw Bobby Jones complaining when others jostled and held him. Before his pro career began he learned some deep lessons about fairness in the 1972 Olympics. Jones played on the United States basketball team that was robbed of a gold medal when the time-keeper refused to tick off the final seconds of the game until their opponents finally scored a basket to beat them. All the moaning in the world wouldn't bring back the gold medal. Jones discovered that the only thing he could do about injustice and cheating was to work harder.

Despite battles with seizures and heart problems,

Jones worked hard enough so that he could play better defense cleanly than others could with all their tricks. From the day he joined the pros in 1974 until his body started slowing down 10 years later, Jones was named to the First Team All-Defensive Unit every year. Four times he was named to the NBA All-Star team, and in 1983 he won the NBA's Sixth Man Award as the best reserve in the game. That was also the year that the 76ers caught some of his work habits and swept to the NBA championship.

Jones's best moves might not spark much attention in a highlight film but they would draw a standing ovation at a coach's clinic. One coach commented that Jones automatically did the things you had to beg other players to do. He didn't mind laboring in the shadows while flashier players drew the attention. There was as much satisfaction to be gained from preventing a breakaway layup as from a cartwheeling slam dunk. Computers don't award style points, and during one season a computer analysis of all NBA players showed that Jones was the most effective. In accepting an award from a liquor company for that achievement, Jones typically stuck to his beliefs and quietly mentioned to the audience he did not endorse the use of their product.

The day never did come when Jones had to hold on to play defense. He went down battling as hard as ever, with a grinding, seven-game play-off series against the Milwaukee Bucks in 1986. Following the heart-breaking, one-point loss in the final game, Jones might have complained about the painful finish to his career. Instead he expressed his happiness that if he had to go out on a losing note, there was no one he would rather lose to than respected Milwaukee coach Don Nelson.

Bobby Jones left the NBA just as he had entered it: genuine, decent, and honest. The only thing he had to rearrange in his life was his trophy case.

Read Exodus 32:21-24,35 for the tragic story of a man who went along with what everyone else was doing. Read James 4:17 to find out what Jones understood better than Aaron did. Then turn to Matthew 5:5-6 for another opinion on where "nice guys" finish.

Winning Isn't Everything

1

At high noon, spectators began to trickle into the Silver Dome in Pontiac, Michigan. If everything went well, within the hour they would be watching the Lions devour the gladiators from Minnesota in this early season football contest in 1976. For this game, desperation and frustration would fuel an especially intense crowd. In each of the past seven years, the Detroit Lions had finished second in their division, and usually it had been the Minnesota Vikings who had knocked them out of the playoffs. After all this time, a little revenge would warm the blood.

At about that time, the Vikings' bus was crawling along the freeway, caught in the quagmire of a traffic jam. Coach Bud Grant didn't like his team killing time at the stadium; his policy was to arrive an hour before game time. Right on schedule, the bus had left the hotel at 11:45, for the 15 minute jaunt to the stadium. Unfortunately, the driver had made a wrong turn.

At 12:15 Detroit coach Rick Forzano went over last-minute preparations for the game knowing full well there had better not be any slip-ups. The endless ordeal of "close but no cigar" in the Central Division had frayed the nerves of the Lions' owner. Although this was only Forzano's second full season as coach of the team, jumpy Detroit management was ready to pounce at the first signs of trouble. Detroit's offense had sputtered in both of their first two games, and although they had won one of them, rumors were flying that Forzano had better come up with more points or he was gone. The strain of pressure was taking its toll on the players as well as Forzano, and tempers were running high on the team. As the beleaguered coach surveyed the filling stands he could hardly help but notice something was missing. Where were the Vikings?

Unknown to him, the Vikings were parked in a sea of stalled metal on the Detroit freeway. Traffic accidents had further snarled the flow so that in the next half hour, the bus could only advance three quarters of a mile. Now, stuck again in a cloverleaf intersection a quarter mile from the stadium, it was obvious that the Vikings were going to miss the 1:05 kick-off time, something that had never happened in the history of televised pro football. Desperately, some of them got off the bus to ask other cars to move for them, and the bus tightroped along the narrow shoulder of the road to get to the stadium.

Detroit fans buzzed in amazement as 1:05 arrived before the Vikings did. Network and NFL executives frantically scrambled to fill the air time that was supposed to be bringing pro football into living rooms across the country. Amid all the swirling confusion of a situation that no one had ever planned for, Rick Forzano kept his head. It would have been easy to gloat about the Vikings' misfortune, about their penalty for being late, and about their lack of warm-up time. There was a good chance the Lions could jump on the Vikings while they were still cold and build a quick lead.

But as Paul Krause led the Vikings on to the field at 1:07, the Detroit coach approached the officials who were still trying to decide how to reschedule the starting time. Forzano admitted to them that this was a game he badly wanted to win. But he pointed to the great athletes on the Vikings' squad, All-Pros like Carl Eller, Alan Page, Fran Tarkenton, and Chuck Foreman. Without proper time to warm up, these men left themselves wide open to serious injury that could endanger their careers. "If I were Coach Grant I would appreciate an extra 10 minutes to warm up. It's OK with me if you can arrange that."

Following the 1:27 kickoff, the teams flailed away at each other without scoring in the first half. In the second half the Vikings finally staked out a 10–3 lead and held it until two minutes to go when Detroit tight end Charlie Sanders corralled a touchdown pass from Greg Landry.

Unfortunately the extra point was blocked. Once again Minnesota had narrowly escaped the clutches of the Detroit Lions. The blame for the 10-9 defeat fell on Rick Forzano, who resigned a week later. The smallest edge might have been enough to finally pin the Vikings to the wall that day, but when the chance had come Forzano had turned it down rather than gain it at the expense of the Viking players.

2

In the spring of 1985, you could plunge the most cheerful, bubbly Minnesotan into a fog of gloom by saying two short words: "Ron Davis." Many Twins' fans held that the one thing that could be done to most improve the quality of life in the state would be to trade Davis. Ever since he had come over from the Yankees, packaged as the Twins new bullpen ace, the six-foot four-inch man with the explosive sidearm fastball had been a target of abuse. Well-deserved abuse, in the opinion of many. Here was a man who was spilling over with talent, who had already pitched in the All-Star game and the World Series games. The Twins had finally cracked into their savings account to pay the high salary that a star like Davis commanded only to find that he wasn't worth any more than his bargain basement teammates. Bringing Ron Davis in to protect a late-inning lead was like diving into a tent for protection against a tornado. Sometimes the lead survived but often it didn't, and Davis's war of words with management branded him as a spoiled kid with a bad attitude.

It took only a few aggravating squandered leads before Davis won the title of public enemy number one among Twins fans. His successes were quickly tucked out of mind to be forgotten completely the next time he snatched defeat from the jaws of victory. By the Twins' home opener in 1985, hating Ron Davis had become the latest fad. While the other Twins were cheered, the bespectacled reliever was loudly booed when introduced with his family before the game.

For awhile, Ron shouldered the boos as a hazard of his job. But under the surface, the mocking tones were chipping away at his confidence. On a road trip to the East Coast, that weakened confidence shattered. Still smarting from the taunts suffered after allowing a ninth inning home run to lose a game early in the year, Davis came in to protect a narrow lead against Baltimore. The Orioles' Fred Lynn greeted him with a ninth inning home run that cost the Twins the game.

Other Twins relievers had no better luck keeping the ball in the park. With Davis looking on in sympathy, they lost the very next game on another ninth inning homer.

Determined to weave a comfortable cushion that could stand up to these late inning follies, Minnesota hitters blasted the New York Yankees in the early innings of their May 13 contest. With an 8–0 lead after two innings, they settled back from their labors certain that not even their jittery pitching staff could waste that lead. But by the eighth inning the lead had slipped to 8–6. For lack of a better solution, Davis was called in to douse a Yankee rally. This time Davis answered the call by striking out slugger Dave Winfield to end the inning. Regaining confidence with each pitch, Davis coasted through the eighth inning without allowing a run.

In the ninth, Ron walked the first Yankee batter but recovered to retire the next two men. Only one more out was needed to nail down the win and halt the Twins' horrendous losing streak. Bearing down with all his might, Davis fired some scorching pitches but his location was off center. The batter walked, bringing up New York's top hitter, Dale Mattingly. Fighting back the tension, Davis breathed deeply and threw. The crack of the bat must have sounded like a hammer driving a stake into his heart. The recurring nightmare had come back to haunt him as Mattingly lofted the pitch into the seats for a home run that sent the Yanks away with a 9–8 win, and sent Davis into a near breakdown.

Interviewed in the Twins' dugout after the game, Davis fought back tears. "I'm a disgrace," he said. Bewildered, anguished, Davis dressed in a daze, his life devastated by the pain of being the laughingstock of a whole state. Twins fans had jumped all over him before—the letters, the jeers, the unending boos. What would they do now in the face of these latest humiliations? "I know I'm going to get killed when I go back home," he muttered.

As the "Dump on Ron Davis" fad bubbled towards the boiling point, a Minneapolis sports columnist dug up some interesting, little-known facts about the lanky fastballer. A while back Davis had come to the Twins' public relations people and volunteered to give inner-city kids a chance to fish. Footing the entire bill himself, Davis had rented a bus and, working through a boys club, had filled it with kids eager to try their luck. Instead of an image of a surly pitcher blowing leads on the mound, Twins fans were shown a picture of a man running himself ragged, baiting hooks, yanking off fish, and laughing and fooling around with the kids.

When it was all over, Davis had asked to organize more such outings. Furthermore, Twins officials confirmed that whenever a special case came up where someone was needed to visit the sick or do other charitable work, Davis was the first person they turned to.

That was all very nice, but it didn't win baseball games. Davis steeled himself for the worst when the Twins returned home to face the Detroit Tigers on May 16. He even asked his wife to stay home to spare her the pain of what would happen if he entered the game. Throughout most of the contest, though, it seemed Davis would ride out the evening safely hidden in the bullpen. Ken

Schrom appeared to need no help as he tossed a five-hitter through eight innings and carried a 7–1 lead into the ninth.

But the Twins' ninth-inning jinx claimed another victim. A single and home run closed the gap to 7–3. The home fans grew jittery. Another home run, 7–4. A double. Cheers and encouragement from the stands was being choked off. It was obvious that someone was going to have to bail out Schrom and the fans knew too well the game-saving record of the bullpen crew. The call came for Ron Davis.

Bracing himself for the torrent of boos, Davis started toward the mound. He was at their mercy now. He couldn't even bluff his way through with defiance or arrogance because he believed he deserved whatever they gave him. But as Davis took the mound, an unfamiliar noise echoed through the stadium. As he stood in utter disbelief, 22,000 fans rose to their feet, their applause growing until it thundered off the roof and walls and drowned out every other sound.

Pumped up by the deafening roar of approval, Davis struck out the first batter, then allowed a double. A few days ago that might have been enough to pop his confidence. But the right-hander had received a transfusion of confidence from the crowd. Flinging the ball with a fierce determination, he got dangerous Lou Whitaker to swing awkwardly at a changeup for the game-winning strikeout.

It was a reborn Ron Davis who walked proudly to the mound in the late innings the rest of the season. The chorus of boos that had greeted him during every home game turned to cheers and chants of "R-D, R-D!" For the rest of the season Ron Davis became the intimidating force that scouts had predicted he could become. Striking out 72 batters in 64 2/3 innings, Davis saved 20 of the 21 close games in which he pitched. Once the scapegoat for the Twins' problems, Davis was voted the team's Most Valuable Player for the year.

Of all the great moments in baseball history, could there have ever been a catch, a home run, or a key strikeout that could compete with the moment when 22,000 fans surprised a beaten Ron Davis and poured out the applause that let him now feel that despite his frustrations, he still was immensely valuable as a human being?

Read Luke 12:16-21 for the story of a man who thought that being number one was everything. Then read 1 Timothy 6:11 to find the higher goal that Forzano and the Metrodome fans zeroed in on.

We Have Met the Enemy

1

It was a game so meaningless the score wasn't even reported in some major newspapers around the country. The 66,000 fans who chose to spend this December 3, 1972, afternoon watching the hometown Kansas City Chiefs did so mostly out of habit. For the first time in years, play-off fever had skipped Kansas City. Fans were only kidding themselves if they thought the stadium would be rocking when the slumping Chiefs (5–6) played out the string against the traditionally inept Denver Broncos (3–8).

By the middle of the fourth quarter, most of them had left. If the mushy lack of tension hadn't discouraged them, two hours of shivering in rain and snow fanned by chill winds had.

But for the giants slogging in the trenches, it was no yawning affair. The grunts and explosions from relentless high-speed collisions could turn the strongest stomach queasy. By the fourth quarter, the sloppy field had reduced the speed of the banging bodies, but the slipperiness sent the limbs of the soggy contestants flying out at precarious angles.

Denver had surprised the favored Chiefs by running out to a lead and now were trying to hold back a Kansas City rally in the final quarter. As always, veteran running back Floyd Little led the Bronco charge. The defending NFL rushing champion scampered through a small crack in the Chiefs towering defensive line and lurched downfield for a long gain before he disappeared under a panting, red-jerseyed gang of tacklers.

Suddenly there was a scream. Twisted under a mountain of bodies, Floyd Little's knee had been stretched in a direction God never intended for it to go. Helplessly caught in the tangle, Kansas City linebacker Jim Lynch saw what had happened. In that instant Floyd Little had ceased to be the enemy and had become a person who needed help. "He's hurt!" Lynch yelled to a Kansas City teammate. "I'll hold him while you get everyone off!"

Gingerly, the Chiefs peeled players off the pile until Little was free. Beside them was Kansas City coach Hank Stram who had rushed onto the field at the first report of Little's injury, his face etched with concern. Rather than leaving the Broncos to tend to their own problems, Lynch and 285-pound Kansas City tackle Buck Buchanan tenderly lifted the great running back and carried him to the Bronco bench. Having done all they could do, the Chiefs put their helmets back on and returned to their job, struggling to a 24–21 victory.

2

No one could have prepared Jesse Owens for this moment. Did anyone know what it was like for a black man to stand in a walled stadium crammed with screaming fans in the middle of Nazi Germany? Could anyone have described how it would feel to run under the stare of Adolph Hitler, knowing that he was personally spoiling The Fuhrer's elaborate party?

Already in these 1936 Olympic Games, Owens had exploded Hitler's showcase of his "master race" by sweeping to victory in the 100-meter dash. Now, on August 5th, Owens was preparing to strike two more blows at his host. While also running preliminary heats of the 200-meter dash, Owens would be aiming for victory in his best event, the long jump. Only a year earlier, the "Buckeye Bullet" had soared to a world record with a leap of 26 feet, 8-¼ inches. In these Olympics there was only one man capable of challenging him, Luz Long of Germany. No doubt Long would be especially primed to stop Owens's irritating winning in front of the German home crowd.

The 22-year-old Owens seemed to be bearing up well under the strain until the start of the long jump preliminaries. Certain that it was his last chance to fine-tune his approach, Owens pounded down the track toward the take-off board and then ran through the pit so as not to waste a jump. Officials, however, claimed that the competition had started. That would count as Owens's first jump, and would be recorded as a foul.

That left Owens with two more chances to make a qualifying leap. There was still no need to break a sweat; anything over 23 feet would get him to the finals, and Owens could do that jumping off the wrong leg. He sprinted down the runway on his second attempt but misjudged the distance to the takeoff board. His toe crossed over the line and another foul was declared.

Now Owens was in deep trouble. His timing was off

and there would be no more chances to make the necessary adjustments. With legs half-spent from a tough 200-meter preliminary heat, his confidence was shaken.

Just before Owens was to take that last jump, Luz Long walked up to Owens and introduced himself. "Why don't you put a mark on this side of the board and aim for that," Long suggested. "That way you'll be sure not to foul and you'll still be able to jump far enough to get to the finals.

Taking the advice, Owens scratched a line nearly a foot behind the take-off board. Free from the worry that he might inch over the board and be disqualified, Owens made the finals with a jump of just over 24 feet.

With six chances in the final round, Owens did not have to worry so much about making a mistake. On his second jump, he flew over the pit to an Olympic record of 25 feet, 9-¾ inches. Germany's Long matched that with a tremendous effort on his fifth chance. Spurred on by the competition, Owens then topped that on both of his final jumps, finishing with a gold-medal winning 26 feet, 5-¼ inch. Long took the silver medal.

Instead of sullenly brooding about his defeat, Long seemed to have genuinely enjoyed the excitement of the competition. Ignoring the Nazi doctrine of racial superiority, Long congratulated Owens and walked around the track with him. The two became close friends for the rest of the Olympics.

Owens never saw his friendly rival after the Olympics, however. World War II broke out three years later and among its victims was a German soldier named Luz Long. Forty-eight years after the Olympic competition, the feats of Jesse Owens returned to national attention when Carl Lewis matched his record of four gold medals

in a single Olympic track and field competition. Almost
buried in the footnotes of history was the story of the
enemy without whose sportsmanship that record might
never have been possible.

*Long and the Kansas City Chiefs are two examples of
the law of love that goes a step farther than what comes
naturally to most people. Read Luke 6:31-35 to find out
what this law is.*

Vengeance Is Mine

Roosevelt Grier was a good man to have on your team. For starters he stood six feet five inches, and even under the most severe of diets he still chased the scale right up to the 300-pound mark. That bulk wasn't just for show, either; Grier liked to keep it in motion. Aggressive, fearless, and fast on his feet, Roosevelt anchored the defensive line for the powerful New York Giants in the late 1950s, and went on to become the largest member of the Los Angeles Rams' legendary Fearsome Foursome in the 1960s.

You didn't have to hide the kids or shove the family dog out of the way when Grier was around, either. The one criticism that stuck to the man during his playing career was that he wasn't mean enough. This gentle giant loved needlework as much as butting heads on the field. To him the joy of football was not the satisfaction of a crunching tackle but the feeling of togetherness as a team strove to reach a common goal. Grier even used the word *love* to talk about a team.

When a severe leg injury bounced Grier out of the Fearsome Foursome, Grier immediately began singing the praises of his replacement, Roger Brown. After grueling exercises failed to bring his leg back in fighting shape,

Grier gave up on football in 1968. There was no question, however, of him moping around, mourning his lost profession. Grier couldn't sit still if he wanted to, he was always out looking for more of the joy of life. Before long he was singing, playing guitar, and drawing up the plans for his own local television show in Los Angeles.

One of the few things that seemed safe from Roosevelt's enthusiasm was politics. There just didn't seem to be a lot of joy to be squeezed from that quarrelsome arena of life. But when friends such as former Olympic champion Rafer Johnson and retired Eagle running back Timmy Brown asked him to help out in the campaign of Robert F. Kennedy, Grier agreed. Grier had once worked with Kennedy on a fund-raising task and had been impressed. Of course, Grier couldn't just dip his toe in any new water; he plunged his huge heart and soul into the campaign. He saw Bobby Kennedy as a great man and a persuasive leader. There was no one more sincere in persuading voters that here was a leader whom a person could really believe in.

The night before one of Grier's first television tapings, Robert Kennedy was in Los Angeles after taking his case to the California voters. All the hands had been shaken, all the phone calls made in the primary campaign, and now it was time to await the results. Among those who spent that evening with the presidential hopeful was Grier.

In a hotel ballroom teeming with reporters and well-wishers, Kennedy presented his final speech and forged his way through the throng toward the door. A powerful man could always be useful in such circumstances and Grier escorted Kennedy's wife Ethel to protect her from jostling. They made their way safely outside the ballroom door when Grier suddenly heard a gunshot. Instinctively, he pushed Ethel to the floor out of harm's way and raced toward Senator Kennedy.

In an instant he saw his bleeding friend and the man who had shot him, gun still in hand. Grier grabbed the gunman in a bear hug and pried the weapon loose from his hand. Lifting him in his great arms, he threw Sirhan Sirhan onto a table and held him down.

In the heat of rage and despair, Roosevelt Grier could have torn Sirhan apart with his bare hands. Many enraged onlookers were of a mind to do just that and they swarmed over to the table to get at the assassin. Had the giant athlete not stood in their path, they might have taken their vicious revenge. But Grier spread his huge form over Sirhan and shielded him from the fists and clutching hands. Blow after blow rained down on Grier but he held his ground. When the mob was finally pulled back, there was Roosevelt Grier, tears streaking his normally cheerful face, crying for the loss of his friend while protecting the man who killed him.

"Too many people have been killed in this country," said Grier, who was later a pallbearer at Kennedy's funeral. Thanks to Grier the world was spared at least one bit of mindless violence, so that even in painful circumstances, vengeance could be replaced by justice.

Read Luke 22:47-51 for an example of how someone else protected an enemy from violence at the hands of his own friends. Then go to Romans 12:19 for advice about getting revenge.

Spread It Around

A classic cliche in sports lore: the kid lies dying in the hospital, his will to live broken. Into the room walks a slugger such as Babe Ruth, who chucks the kid under the chin and promises to hit a home run just for him. The superstar does it and the kid, inspired, miraculously recovers.

Is that the truth or just some Hollywood sob story? Like much that surrounded the wild and blustery world of Babe Ruth, the original story was a confection made of equal parts fiction and fact. But don't let that harden your skepticism about athletes and their efforts to give something back to a world that gives them so much. The real stories happen every day and they don't need the Hollywood tear-jerking hype to touch us.

Milwaukee Bucks coach Don Nelson reads a letter from a financially-strapped fan about to lose his farm, then donates his entire play-off check to the desperate farmer. Baltimore Oriole slugger Eddie Murray signs a check for $500,000 to establish a youth camp in Baltimore. Indiana Pacer forward Clark Kellogg conducts basketball clinics for the retarded and donates hundreds of tickets for them to attend Pacer games. Miami Dolphin center Dwight Stephenson volunteers time at a home for babies with health problems. Yankee outfielder Dave Winfield sets up a scholarship for young student-athletes and puts on a massive All-Star Game party for 15,000 underprivileged children. Mark Eaton, the seven-foot, five-inch center of the Utah Jazz donates five dollars for every shot he blocked to an association for the deaf.

A semi-truck load of medals could easily be passed out among pro athletes and coaches. But here, briefly, are five selected cases of pro stars spreading it around:

1

So maybe it didn't happen quite the way legend has it. Little Johnny Sylvester *was* sick and in the hospital, and Babe Ruth *did* stop by to visit him. Johnny *did* ask Babe to swat a home run for him, and Ruth *did* clout a round-tripper the next game. But Johnny wasn't deathly ill, and Ruth wasn't doing him any special favors. The Babe was always promising to try and hit a home run for someone. When the story was later brought to his attention, Ruth didn't have the slightest idea who Johnny Sylvester was!

The discovery that the story is partly counterfeit, however, cannot blot out the fact the Ruth's appetite for generosity was as enormous as his appetite for food and parties. If the Yankee home run king couldn't remember his chat with Johnny, it was because he visited too many people to keep track of.

Ruth hated hospitals and would often come home from them feeling depressed and listless. Yet whenever he was approached, he would promise to go, without even finding out where the hospital was. After asking Yankee officials to locate the hospital, Ruth would go out for a night on the town. The Babe could outlast almost everyone at a party, but even if he finally straggled home two minutes before an early morning hospital appointment, he would show up on time, at bedside, greeting the patient with a smile.

Once in his later years, the record-setting Sultan of Swat was so sick he could barely walk, yet he fulfilled his promise to appear at a charity golf tournament. After dragging himself around in agony for a few holes, the blinding pain forced him to drop out of the tournament. No sooner had he hobbled off the course than someone had the nerve to ask him to visit a blind friend. Without hesitation, Babe Ruth limped off on another mission of mercy.

2

Young Brett Butler had barely begun patrolling center field for the Atlanta Braves in 1982 but already he had won the hearts of a legion of Braves' fans. Showing flashes of the brilliance that in 1985 would propel him among the top 10 in his league in batting average, hits, runs, stolen bases, and triples, he had especially drawn the gaze of a 10-year-old Atlanta girl.

When the cruel diagnosis came that one of the girl's legs was so badly damaged that it must be amputated, her mother searched for a way to ease her pain. She remembered that when the girl had written a fan letter to Butler, the baseball player had answered promptly and politely. Ringing up the Braves' offices, she asked if Butler could possibly call her daughter on the phone to get her mind off the operation for awhile.

The request was relayed to Butler, who remembered the letter. He decided that the girl's plight required more than a phone call. Off he went to Scottish Rite Hospital and spent three hours talking with his little fan. According to Atlanta publicity director Wayne Minshew, "I don't know what you say to a youngster who is about to lose a leg at the height of the playground and fun and games stages of her life, but Brett apparently did."

According to the grateful mother, the visit worked wonders. Instead of sinking into depression, the girl's spirits were lifted and she made it through the operation in great shape.

Such journeys into the deepest reaches of emotion are no safer for athletes than for anyone else. Butler was so touched by his visit that he didn't play well for a few games. But somehow, out of the range of cameras and newsmen, he felt moved to do what he could.

3

On a cold January afternoon in 1980, nine-year-old Cory Gurnsey of Calgary, Alberta, walked home from school, warmed by his most prized possession. It wasn't just any old red, white, and blue Montreal Canadiens' sweater he was wearing, his was stamped with number 10. Any hockey fan knew that this number belonged to Guy Lafleur, the man who was called by one rival goalie "by far the greatest shooter of our time."

Although only nine, Cory had been leading the cheers

for Lafleur for years. He could tell you all about those six seasons from 1974–1975 to 1979–1980 during which Lafleur scored more than fifty goals each year and led the Canadiens to three straight Stanley Cup titles. Wearing a replica of his hero's uniform, Cory felt invincible.

Unfortunately, the uniform's magic could not ward off the attack of a crazed assailant. A knife-wielding man jumped him before he reached home, stabbed him repeatedly, and left him to die. In the hospital emergency room, doctors had to cut away the sweater in order to get at the near-fatal wounds. For Cory, the pain and horror of the attack was bad enough, but the loss of his sweater was too much.

A reporter then phoned the Montreal team and asked if they could send a replacement jersey. They did better than that. Cory was still struggling in intensive care when word came that a new number 10 jersey with Lafleur's name on the back, an autographed picture of Lafleur, and a phone call from the great right-winger were coming soon.

Lafleur had heard of the old Babe Ruth legend and decided to give it a shot when he called the fast-improving youngster. "Watch our next televised game and I'll score a goal for you," he promised. Sure enough, Lafleur lived up to his promise and had the goal-scoring puck mounted on a plaque.

But the best part was yet to come. When Cory was strong enough to travel, some Calgary people arranged to fly him to Montreal to meet Lafleur. There he was given a seat behind the Canadiens' bench where he could talk to Lafleur and be one of the first to congratulate him on his goal against the Vancouver Canucks.

Within two months, Cory was back in school. A strong

dose of caring on the part of Lafleur and the Canadiens had smoothed the way to recovery.

4

Joe Jacoby had already lost his mother, father, and brother. But even with the pain of those losses, the All-Pro tackle for the Washington Redskins did not shy away from another brutally painful confrontation with death.

William David Newkirk III was fighting with all his might against a deadly cancer, but he needed help. The 300-pound Jacoby, who had blasted paths through the Miami Dolphin defense to lead the Redskins to victory in the 1983 Super Bowl had the strength and the compassion to give it to him.

No one knows what was said during those many secret phone calls from a Redskin star to his team's most ardent fan that year, but whatever it was, it helped the nine-year-old boy to suffer the pain and worry cheerfully. David was never seen without his Redskins' baseball cap, provided by Jacoby. It was the boy's belief that some Redskin magic in the cap could keep him from losing too much hair during months of radiation treatment.

Big Joe escorted his little friend to the Redskin locker room after an exhibition game against Kansas City. Calling it the happiest day of his life, David collected a scrapbook of all the details of his visit and leafed through it time after time in his room. He laughed when Jacoby let him try on his Super Bowl ring and found that it overflowed two of his fingers together. He cried when the Skins lost the next Super Bowl and loyally bragged that Joe was the only Redskin who had played great.

Shortly thereafter, David lost his one-sided war to cancer. He was buried in a Redskin sweater. It had been a cruelly short stay on earth for the boy but because Jacoby had not backed away from the pain of losing another friend, the boy had savored some of life's sweetest moments.

5

Magic Johnson, the fast break wizard with the boyish grin who has made basketball fun for the Los Angeles Lakers, carries his high-spirited act wherever he goes. Among the recipients of a Magic dose of sunshine was a Pittsburgh boy named Joe Hill. The "Make a Wish" Foundation contacted Magic and said that the boy was dying of leukemia and had told them that the one thing he most wanted to do in the world was to meet Magic. Johnson and the Lakers agreed to do what they could.

Magic Johnson, who on the basketball court seems to welcome pressure as a sail welcomes a brisk wind, finally had run into something that was almost too much for him. The night before Joe arrived, Magic couldn't sleep. After tossing and turning trying to think of eloquent things to say to his visitor, Magic decided to just be himself.

The next day Magic met his fan and shot baskets with him. At lunch the Laker star informed him that he wasn't going to just sit and watch the game that night. "I'm putting you to work!" Magic said. For one evening in his short life, which was to end in a few months, Joe Hill became part of the Lakers, the ball boy. Although his obligation to the boy was more than complete, Magic took the entire Hill family to dinner the next night.

It was the way that Johnson worked his charitable magic more than the deeds themselves that often made the difference. During 1983 training camp, Johnson, who liked to keep his volunteer work secret, agreed to a woman's request that he visit a training center for retarded adults. He wasn't supposed to do that during camp, but figured he could squeeze it in during the monotony of training.

The morning of the scheduled visit, Laker coach Pat Riley canceled practice. Since it would be his only day off to get away from the grueling training camp, Magic was given the option of backing out of the visit. Magic saw that the unexpected break was indeed an opportunity, but one of a different nature. "No," he said. "Now I won't be in a rush when I go there."

Read 2 Corinthians 9:6-7 to find out what was so special about the attitude of the athletes in this chapter.

Created Equal

1

On the surface Branch Rickey's grand experiment was proceeding steadily, if warily, through its many obstacles. But two menacing underground movements threatened to sabotage the Brooklyn general manager's determination to break the color barrier and put a black ballplayer in a Dodger uniform. A core group of racists on the Dodgers began to circulate a petition protesting the inclusion of Jackie Robinson on the 1947 roster, while in St. Louis, the Cardinals made plans to go on strike rather than play on the same field with a black man.

National League president Ford Frick got wind of the Cardinal plot and quickly defused it by pronouncing judgment in advance; anyone who refused to play against the Dodgers would face suspension. The internal threat among the Dodgers, however, was a little trickier, and posed a special dilemma for shortstop Pee Wee Reese. Although Reese swung a potent bat as well as anchored the Dodger defense, it was rumored that Robinson had been groomed to take over Reese's position.

The Kentucky-born Reese brushed off the rumors,

mainly because of ignorance. He had never really met a black man. All he knew about them was what he had been told, and the word was that blacks couldn't handle pressure the way white players could. Talented as Robinson seemed to be, Reese didn't expect him to survive in the big leagues. But the pressure built for Reese to sign the petition. According to the way he had been brought up, whites and blacks weren't supposed to mix. Black people had been banned from playing in the park where Reese learned his baseball. Reese's family let him know that this business of playing with black players bothered them.

Reese was a key man in the drive to get rid of Robinson. After all, he was a leader, one of the team's most respected names. But when the paper was presented to him to sign, Reese refused. That ended any talk of mutiny on the Dodgers.

To Reese's surprise, Robinson not only stuck with the club but earned the major league's Rookie of the Year Award. Instead of replacing Reese, Robinson complimented him by playing alongside Pee Wee in the Dodger infield at second base. Reese acted as though there was nothing at all unusual about Robinson playing for the Dodgers. He never went out of his way to be nice to him, an honest brand of acceptance which Robinson later said he appreciated more than anything else.

A year was far from enough, however, to douse long-burning embers of prejudice. During a 1948 game the Boston Braves showered ridicule on Reese for stooping so low as to play alongside a black. Giving no indication that he could even hear them, Reese strode over to Robinson and put his hand on his teammate's shoulder. No one remembers what idle chatter passed between the two. But not only did it shut up the Braves for the rest of the game, it helped to forge a lasting friendship between two fine infielders.

2

There are few honors white South Africa can bestow that equals the awarding of a Springbok jersey given to those who earn a spot on the national rugby team. Cheeky Watson voluntarily exchanged that honor for a lifetime of harassment and intimidation.

In 1976 Watson approached the very top rungs of the ladder in the South African rugby world when he was selected to the junior Springbok team that was to play archrival New Zealand. At about that time he was asked if he would help coach a newly organized local black team. Although South Africa's laws strictly separate blacks and whites and bar blacks from taking part in the government, Watson agreed.

When he discovered the hardships the blacks faced just to play a little rugby, he was jolted into action. It was ridiculous for the blacks to have to practice under the headlights of five cars when there were perfectly good, lighted fields for whites nearby. Watson tried to draw out support from the members of his own club, the Crusaders, but their answer stopped him cold. No, the blacks couldn't use any of their lighted fields, not even the practice field with the floodlights.

Watson quit the team rather than agree to such a policy and he took his rugby skills to the township to play with the black team. The star athlete's action embarrassed officials of the sport who tried to coax him away from his stand by offering him a spot on the Springboks for an approaching tour in France. But in light of what he had seen, the lure of the Springbok jacket lost its hold on him. Even when officials raised the stakes of his program by targeting him for intimidation, Watson held firm. Watson was arrested and thrown in the back of vans when he was discovered violating the laws that said whites could not be in a black township after 5:00 P.M. Even when he pointed out the blacks had to work in factories all day and could not possibly play before 5:00, he was booked for breaking the law.

Ten years later, still shunned by many whites for his stand against South Africa's laws of racial segregation, Cheeky Watson refused to look back with longing on a heroic athletic career that never was. Without a trace of regret for what might have been he held on to what was more important. "I can sleep at night because I have a clear conscience."

The Samaritans were a group of people that were looked down upon by those around them. Read John 4:7-15,27-30,40 for a story about someone else who did not let prejudice stand in the way. Then look up Galatians 3:28.

But Not Forgotten

1

It looked like an impossible mission; however, Howard Jones had no choice but to accept it. The University of Southern California's 1931 football schedule called for a cross-country trip to Indiana to play Notre Dame. For Southern Cal's Coach Jones, it was a task equal to trying to outbid the Rockefellers at an auction.

The ranks of Notre Dame's Fighting Irish were bursting with such talent that they had captured fans throughout the country and had almost single-handedly turned college football into a major sport. It had been three years since anyone had beaten the Irish; in fact it had been Jones's own Trojans that had last turned the trick back in 1928. This time, though, they would have to beat Notre Dame in its own backyard. Powered by the cheers of their devoted fans, the Irish had lost only one home game in 26 years.

Despite the fact that the Irish were undefeated again this year, Jones felt something missing when his team took the field against them. No longer would he have the pleasure and the frustration of a sideline duel with

Notre Dame's legendary coach, Knute Rockne. Called by many the greatest coach of all time, a master of motivation, Rockne had been killed in late spring when the plane he was traveling in crashed in the fields of Kansas.

For most of the afternoon, it seemed to have been a wasted trip for the Southern Cal Trojans. Despite their fierce, aggressive play, they could not break through the Notre Dame defensive wall. Going into the final period, Notre Dame nursed a 14–0 lead, as well as numerous bruises and bumps from the visitors' reckless tackling.

It was then that the sparks that had been flying all day from the intense Trojans finally burst into flame. Gaius Shaver blasted over for a touchdown following a 47-yard drive. Shrugging off the setback of having their extra point blocked, Howard Jones's men began grinding out another touchdown drive. Fifty-seven yards from where the march began, Shaver again broke through for a score; that closed the gap to 14–13.

Their steel shell of home-field confidence now crumbling around them, the Irish fell back under yet another Trojan assault with four minutes remaining. They surged to the 12 before Notre Dame finally regrouped and threw them for a three-yard loss. When a Southern Cal dropped a pass on the next play, it looked as though, in the final minute, the Irish home field magic had finally bent the Trojans' will.

Having seen what Notre Dame could do to a place-kick attempt, Coach Jones decided to try a field goal on third down rather than wait until fourth down when the Irish would be ready for it. Johnny Baker swung his foot into the ball and it sailed 33 yards through the uprights for the winning score.

Overcome with both relief and joy, the Trojans began

their wild celebration. But Coach Jones, at the moment of the greatest triumph in his career, seemed curiously somber. In the locker room, his players held back their delirium as they sensed their coach's mood. When an award ceremony was set up to present Southern Cal with a trophy as the best college football team in the land, Coach Jones paid no attention to the trophy. Instead he quietly asked if someone could give him directions to a cemetery. Within an hour, the entire Southern California team huddled around the grave of Knute Rockne, adding their silent prayers while their coach paid his respects to a great rival.

2

Indiana University's energetic Bobby Knight owned a reputation for getting the most out of his players, but Landon Turner was putting that reputation in jeopardy. Although blessed with 6-foot, 10-inch, 240-pound size, and speed and grace to match, the Hoosier basketball forward lost playing time in favor of those with a fraction of his ability. Worst of all, Turner's mind didn't always seem to be on what he was doing, and that ranked as one of life's chief sins in Coach Knight's eyes. Not surprisingly, player and coach clashed repeatedly during Turner's first seasons.

Suddenly in the middle of his junior year in 1981, Landon Turner became a basketball player, the kind that even a perfectionist like Knight could be proud of. With Turner taking charge at the power forward spot, a good Indiana team grew into a powerhouse just in time for the NCAA tournament. The new Landon Turner gave Knight a defensive wildcat he could unleash on the opponents' strongest inside player.

Turner surprised highly-rated LSU by holding their ace, Rudy Macklin, scoreless in the second half while scoring a game-high 20 points himself. The result was a 67–49 blowout that left Indiana fresh for the 1981 championship match against North Carolina. The Tar Heels' front line of Sam Perkins, Al Wood, and James Worthy (all later first-round draft choices of the pros) was touted as the most dominating in the game. But Turner, who had started his surge too late to earn much mention in the press, had apparently neglected to read the Tar Heels' press clippings.

After Perkins flipped in seven points to stake North Carolina to a 16–8 lead, Coach Knight gave him the Turner treatment. For the rest of the game, the Tar Heel front line seemed to disappear and Indiana breezed to a 63–50 win.

Based on what he had seen of Turner in the tournament, Knight figured he could count on the first-team All-American returning to lead his squad the next season. A terrifying couple of seconds in late July, however, scrambled that prediction. Driving through the countryside around Bloomington, Indiana, Landon Turner lost control of his car. It veered off the two-lane highway, struck a culvert, and flipped over, leaving Turner crippled.

Never again would he spring high over the hardwood court at Indiana University. But even though Turner's playing days were over, Bobby Knight believed that the word *team* meant more than a collection of bodies playing in the same uniform. Turner was still a part of the team, in fact, he was selected as the squad's captain. Knight didn't want anyone getting the idea it was just an honorary title. When he found the hospital-bound player sporting a few days growth of beard, he made him shave it off, and told him he had work for him to do on the sidelines once he was feeling better. The coach also put his energy into raising the hundreds of thousands of dollars it would take to care for his ex-star during his recovery.

Pro sports is known as a tough business where even stars can be quickly discarded when they no longer produce. But the Boston Celtics showed a more human side of sports the next spring. Celtic general manager Red Auerbach had taken a close look at Turner before the accident and had decided he was the type of hard-working, talented, unselfish player that had made the Celtics the dominant team in pro basketball. During the pro draft of college players, the fans pricked up their ears at Boston's final choice. Disregarding players who might have had an outside chance of helping them, the Celtics made an impossible dream come true by choosing a 6-foot, 10-inch forward from Indiana, Landon Turner. Although unable to walk, Turner's long-time dream of being drafted by the pros had come true.

"We would have been honored to have him on our team," said a Celtic spokesman. "We felt this was one way to show how we felt about him."

"Out of sight, out of mind" is often the way things work. Read Romans 13:7 for an explanation of why it was so important not to forget people like Rockne and Turner.

Self-Respect

1

Who was the best right-handed pitcher in the American League in the late 1970s? If you can answer that Dennis Leonard won more games than any other starboard slinger in the league from 1975–1982, you are in a select company of baseball scholars. Starting each season slower than a car on a subzero night, Leonard was never chosen for the prestigious midseason All-Star game. Yet in an unspectacular, workmanlike fashion, the Kansas City Royals' ace was nearly unbeatable down the backstretch of the pennant races, winning 20 games three times.

In 1983 Leonard finally got out of the gate quickly. By May 28, he had already won six of nine starts and was throwing shutout ball against the Orioles in pursuit of number seven. Facing Baltimore star Cal Ripken in the fourth inning, Leonard felt his left leg snap as he delivered his pitch. Such pain surged through his leg that he rolled over and over on the ground by the mound. Somehow he had ruptured the largest and strongest tendon in the body.

The Royals' ace pitcher had to suffer through four operations just to get the knee patched together. There wasn't any question of resuming his career; no athlete in any sport had ever come back from that type of injury. Fortunately for Leonard, his many years of steady service had paid off at the bargaining table. His contract guaranteed that he would be collecting $800,000 a year for the next 3½ years from the Kansas City club even if he never threw another pitch.

Such high pay for no work may sound like a dream come true for many people but Dennis Leonard couldn't find any peace in that arrangement. Not only did he miss playing baseball, he felt guilty about accepting all that money without earning it. He would not rest until he had tried everything humanly possible to get back into action.

The first time the Kansas City trainer watched Leonard try to jog in 1984, he felt sick. The left leg was so shriveled and wobbly it was hard to imagine Leonard had ever pitched on it. At first Leonard couldn't lift two pounds with that leg. But he gritted his teeth through brutal workouts of biking, jogging, and lifting weights, fighting off the relentless pain. His wife Audrey worried that Dennis was so obsessed with his comeback that he was killing himself. Life for her was hardly easier, either, as she had to do all the work around the house and all the driving, as well as helping tend the knee.

After two and a half years of lonely, seemingly futile workouts, Leonard felt strong enough for the ultimate test. The Royals didn't hold much hope for a 34-year-old pitcher with such a ruined knee being able to regain his form after a two and a half year layoff, but they felt that out of consideration for his efforts, they owed him a chance. Leonard showed them just enough improvement to win one of the last spots on the staff and the plans were to test him as a long reliever in those games when the Kansas City starter was knocked out of the game early.

But when regular starting pitcher Danny Jackson sprained his ankle, the Royals decided it was time to let Leonard sink or swim. Opponents who for a couple of years had wondered whatever happened to Dennis Leonard, suddenly saw him standing on the mound. In the Kansas City dugout Leonard's teammates could hardly stand still as they hoped that by some miracle Leonard could pitch at least close to the way he used to. Although fresh from a harrowingly close World Series clash the previous fall, some Royals claimed that playing in the World Series was like getting a back massage compared to the tension of watching the final test of Leonard's courage.

The Toronto Blue Jays weren't going to be lulled into any sentimental sympathy. Knowing that Leonard still moved awkwardly, they tested his knee in the first inning with a bunt. The Kansas City pitcher passed that test, however, and stunned the crowd of 24,000 with his masterful control. Leonard didn't walk a batter and at one point retired 18 in a row before Tony Fernandez whacked a two-out single in the ninth. Unfortunately, the Kansas City batters had tried so hard to score runs for him that they had tied themselves into knots. As Fernandez took his lead off first base, Toronto trailed only 1–0. Leonard knew that if he gave up one more hit, manager Dick Howser would bring in a reliever. Having come so far, Dennis wanted this to be his game. Striding down hard on the leg that had once failed him so terribly, Leonard struck out Rance Mulliniks to seal his spectacular three-hit shutout.

Even opponents felt moved by the experience. "He could have taken the money and run," they said of Leonard's comeback. Instead, Dennis Leonard was making money the old-fashioned way: he was earning it.

2

No one had batted .400 in the American League in 18 years, but 23-year-old Ted Williams was making a good run for it in 1941. With just six games to go in the season, the third-year man slashed two hits in four at bats to raise his average to .406.

The .400 average, however, was one of baseball's most difficult feats. Most players would happily settle for a 1 for 3 day at the plate. Williams, however, went 1 for 3 in each of the next two games yet saw his average slip to .405.

On a Wednesday doubleheader, the Washington Senators gave him nothing good to hit, and Ted managed only one hit in seven trips, along with two walks. Suddenly his comfortable cushion had disappeared; his batting average had dipped to .401. Newspaper reporters hawking over Ted's .400 challenge sounded the alarm and the pressure grew. At the very end of one of the most successful batting seasons anyone has ever had, Williams's fingernail grip on the magic average seemed to have broken. A one-for-four performance the next game dropped him percentage points below .400.

It was pointed out, however, that his .39955 average would be rounded up to .400 so that Williams could still claim the milestone. Realizing the awful pressure Ted was under and the possible devastation if he would fail on the final day after coming so close, Boston Red Sox manager Joe Cronin offered a solution. The final day's doubleheader versus the Philadelphia A's meant nothing in the standings so he suggested that Williams preserve his .400 average by sitting out.

Although he badly wanted that .400 mark, Williams refused to take the easy way out. "If I can't hit .400 over the full season, I don't deserve it," he said. Reluctantly, Cronin penciled Ted's name onto the lineup card.

Williams quickly dissipated the pressure by blasting four hits in the first game of the twin bill, including his 37th home run. For good measure, he clouted a double and a single in three at bats in the nightcap. The astounding six for eight finish hiked his final average to a resounding .406. In nearly four decades of baseball since then, no one has managed to replace Ted Williams as the last man ever to hit .400. Thanks to Williams's sense of self-respect, baseball fans can remember the last time with pride.

Read Matthew 25:14-28 for the story of one man who played it safe and sat on his talents and two men who dared to make use of theirs. Then turn to Proverbs 22:1 to find out what was worth more to Leonard and Williams than a roomful of trophies

Angels and Servants

1

For some such as Madeline Manning Mims, it takes only a slight steering adjustment, others, such as Terry Cummings, have to crank the wheel with all their might. For a Madeline Manning Mims it seeps in too gently and gradually to notice when it arrives, for a Terry Cummings it is a sheet of lightning ripping open the earth. The stories of these two extra-ordinary athletes illustrate the contrasting ways in which faith can shape lives.

Madeline Manning Mims could easily have been sucked up into the cesspool of despair that surrounded her as she grew up in the Cleveland ghetto. Degrading poverty compounded by severe childhood illnesses could have broken down her defenses against crime and drugs. Her alcoholic father wasn't around often enough to provide her with any guidance through this tough environment.

But just as she surprised doctors with a complete recovery from potentially fatal spinal meningitis, she managed to deflect the corruptions and temptations that brought misery to so many around her. Her not-so-secret armor was her spiritual faith, passed on to her from her mother. Mims remembers sealing quiet bargains with God when she was six years old, offering to do the Lord's work whenever needed.

This inner force found an exciting outlet in high school when she was recruited out of physical education class to run track at John Hay High School in Cleveland. Swiftly making up the gap on far more experienced runners, she was thrown in among top international women runners in a meet in Toronto in February of 1966. Never having run in a crowd before, the panicky high school girl sprinted to the front of the pack to avoid the jostling elbows. By the end of the race, not only was she still in front, she owned the world record in the event!

That exposure opened up a spot for her at the fortress of the United States' top women track athletes, Tennessee State University. Under expert coaching at the school, she fought through torturous workouts, including weeks of high altitude training in New Mexico, to prepare for the 1968 Olympics at Mexico City.

While United States' women had traditionally done well in the sprints, none had ever taken home Olympic gold in the 800-meter race. But the long-legged, five-foot, nine-inch woman from Cleveland showed cagey instincts as well as raw speed and tough conditioning in the Mexico City finals. Shying away from the front-runners for most of the race, she exploded into her finishing kick at just the right time. Her Rumanian and Dutch rivals were left reeling in her wake as she sped to the gold in a time of 2:00.90.

From that peak of success, her interest ebbed and flowed through the years. She retired in 1970 but came back to make the 1972 Olympic team. After another retirement, she came back recharged to again make the U.S. Olympic team in 1976, and set a United States record of 1:57.9 in the half mile.

Back again for the 1980 Olympic Trials, the grand old lady of the middle distances showed the class that earned her the title of team captain on three United States Olympic teams. Just before the 800 final she called all the entrants together to remind them that nobody could lose as long as she did her best. Then the author of the book *Running For Jesus* went out and won the race to earn a spot on her fourth Olympic team.

Since beating the odds in climbing to the top of the sports world, Madeline Manning Mims has felt driven to try and inspire children through her message of dedication, perseverance, and faith. Through all the years of work, heartache, pain, success, and joy, Madeline Manning Mims has insisted that there was one driving force that had given her success and universal respect among her rivals. "I wouldn't be here if it weren't for Jesus Christ."

2

The Robert Tyrell Cummingses of the world don't usually see a lot of blue sky and sunshine. Theirs is a world of darkness, whether the cover of back alley shadows, under the roof of a prison cell, or under three feet of dirt in a graveyard. It took something special to wrench Terry Cummings out from that world into the brightness where he now handles a dual career as a pro basketball star and a minister of the gospel.

The picture of the graceful Rev. Cummings doesn't fit with the pictures of Terry at 16 years of age. One of 13 children of a family struggling to make it on Chicago's north side near the dreaded Cabrini Green housing project area, Cummings seemed to be campaigning—hard among stiff competition in his class—for the "Least Likely to Succeed" title.

Around home Terry was shy, quiet, and secretive, with much to be secretive about. He hated his father and his stern discipline. On the streets he fought against boredom and emptiness in his life by turning into a foulmouthed hood. Terry tried it all, breaking into cars and homes, ripping off Coca-Cola trucks and stealing cash out of safes. Drugs and alcohol were no strangers to the 16-year-old—neither were weapons. In a world where you had to fight or get hurt, Cummings packed a knife and a pistol, and saw blood spilled in more than one gang fight. School was a joke; Cummings's infrequent appearances in the classroom were causing him to flunk out.

During the summer of his 16th year, Cummings was sent just across the border to stay with his grandmother in Hammond, Indiana. His parents hoped the change in scenery would help him settle down. It did more than that. One night when he was trying to sleep, a vision shook him down to the roots of his soul. Cummings awoke terrified, dripping wet, his bed already soaked with sweat and tears.

It may be impossible to clinically describe in detail exactly what happened to Terry Cummings but the result was unmistakable. In an instant he realized he was headed for disaster and needed to change. Terry Cummings awoke with a sanitized vocabulary and a mile of fuse on his formerly quick temper. Returning to classes, he studied hard and improved his grades. Instead of clenching weapons as he strolled through the most dangerous turf in his neighborhood, he carried a Bible, which he read constantly. And not least in importance, as far as the Milwaukee Bucks are concerned, Cummings took up the sport of basketball.

Following three years at DePaul University where he won a reputation for team play and hard work, Cummings moved on to the pros. As a first round draft choice of the San Diego Clippers in 1982 he became the first rookie since Kareem Abdul-Jabbar in 1969 to rank among the NBA's top ten in both scoring and rebounding. Following a trade to the Milwaukee Bucks, the six-foot, nine-inch forward continued to play at an All-Pro level.

Not bad for an ordained minister who was still learning the finer points of his "hobby." Not bad for a small-time hood who was messing up his own life as well as the lives of others. Thanks to a sudden burst of light in the night, many people have been warmed by the glow of a once-cold heart.

Read 2 Timothy 1:5 and Isaiah 6:1-8 for two more contrasting examples of the different ways that people are called into serving God.

The Villain

Watch out for Kermit Washington! Six feet, eight inches, 230 pounds of deadly explosives with a microscopic fuse. Etched deeply into memories of pro basketball fans is the terrifying image of this powerful forward unleashing his psychopathic fury on an unsuspecting opponent.

No one who saw the "highlights" of that early season contest in 1978 between the Los Angeles Lakers and Houston Rockets could forget what happened. The Lakers' Washington, a former first-round draft choice out of American University in Washington, D.C., took up his position as the Lakers' force shield. All around the league, press reports were trumpeting the latest macho addition to the game. Taking their cue from pro hockey's "goon" squads, they talked about "the enforcers," menacing, muscular forwards who could turn an opponent from a raging lion to a docile sheep with their intimidating play. Although counted on to contribute his share of scoring, Kermit Washington played the role of enforcer for Los Angeles. His main job was to provide the inside muscle and threatening glares to keep other teams from converging on and bullying his star teammate Kareem

Abdul-Jabbar. Now in his fifth year, Washington had earned a reputation as one of the strongest, most punishing men in the game.

In this game, friction began building as Houston's seven-foot center Kevin Kunnert and Washington disputed the boundaries between their territory on the court. Before long tempers flared and the two squared off to fight. In an attempt to keep the peace, Houston's four-time All-Star forward Rudy Tomjanovich raced toward them. Just as he arrived, Washington wheeled and hammered him on the face with a wild swing.

Some observers called it "the hardest punch in the history of mankind." The bone structure of Tomjanovich's face was knocked loose from his skull, there were fractures of the face and skull as well as a broken nose and separated upper jaw. Tomjanovich spent two weeks recovering in a hospital and missed the rest of the season.

Immediately angry cries arose demanding that Kermit Washington be banned from pro basketball. He had shown the whole world what kind of a hot and reckless person he was and that type of common criminal didn't belong in a respectable sport. Get the goons out of basketball and give the game back to real athletes! Washington felt the wrath of the sports world and, fearing he would never be allowed to play again, debated taking graduate courses to plan for his new career. After serving a one month suspension, however, Washington was allowed back on the court. As proof of his undesirable character, he was traded in quick succession from Los Angeles to Boston to San Diego to Portland before fading out of the league in 1982.

When you turn over the story of Kermit Washington to the side that never sees the light, however, you see something completely different. Despite the gaudy publicity, Washington was never a goon. Laker coach Jerry West said he was one of the best people he knew, and others described him as a gentle, caring family man. In the words of a Laker official, "Washington was and remains the kindest, most compassionate person I have met in professional sports, or anywhere, for that matter."

In the Lakers' eyes, it was a cruel case of both Tomjanovich and Washington being in the wrong place at the wrong time. Rather than the vicious brawler he was supposed to be, Washington found fights to be frightening. When he saw an angry Kunnert challenge him to blows and he then saw the blur of a second opponent rushing in from the side, he panicked and lashed out not in hatred but fear. After seeing what he had done to Tomjanovich, it happened, it was many nights before he could sleep.

Lost in the drama of one second of violence is the story of the end of Kermit Washington's career. Hobbled by an endless parade of nagging injuries, the big forward could not make it through the 1981–1982 season. In January he retired.

After sitting out for several months however, Washington longed for one more chance to play the game he loved. While many fellow pros were negotiating million dollar contracts, Washington wasn't interested in money. He offered to play for the Portland Trail Blazers for the minimum league salary, which was around $45,000. Of that total, he planned to give away $1000 at each Trail Blazer home game to a needy family in the Portland area. Since the team had 41 scheduled home games, that figured out to $41,000 for charity, meaning that Washington would ask only $4000 for his services!

Unfortunately, the injuries would not release him from

their grip, and Kermit was unable to make the Trail Blazer team. But that didn't stop him from following through on part of his plan. Although he had played in Portland only two and a half years, he showed his concern for people of the area by setting up "The Sixth Man Foundation." Still in existence today, this organization provides compassionate relief for struggling families in the city.

Social scientists tell us that so often people live up to our expectations of them. Kermit Washington, however, managed to avoid the trap. Although he is probably doomed to live on in history as one of pro basketball's worst villains, he hasn't let that stop him from being the caring, compassionate person that he wants to be.

Read Luke 18:9-14 for a story of a "good" person and a "villain." Then turn to Matthew 7:1 for some instructions to consider whenever you are tempted to condemn someone for their actions.

The Greatest Gift of All

The best of pro football's new wave running backs was off duty in Monroe, Louisiana. Sitting in Chenault Park on a hot June day in 1983, Joe Delaney found no hulking brutes to dodge, no blind side shots to endure, no speedsters to outrun. That would all start in a few weeks when Delaney went back to work for the Kansas City Chiefs. Then he would turn on the speed that had once helped capture an NCAA championship in the 400-meter relay. He would reach deep within himself for the courage and elusiveness that he had shown in setting four Kansas City rushing records, including the Chiefs' single season mark of 1,121 yards, which he gained in 1981 in only 234 carries.

Despite those achievements, Joe Delaney could still sit alone on a park lawn and not attract swarms of celebrity-seekers. The farm boy from Haughton, Louisiana, had gained little recognition at unheralded Northwest Louisiana State University. Standing only 5 feet, 10 inches tall, and weighing 184 pounds, anemic by pro football standards, he had been bypassed by the fanfare that accompanies all first round selections, and was quietly taken by the Chiefs in the second round. He wasn't one to stand up in a crowd and beat his chest, either.

But after such feats as an 82-yard touchdown run against Houston boosted him into the Pro Bowl as a rookie, Delaney could expect that his moments of peace in a public place were about to become only memories. A man with his work habits could only improve, if he didn't burn himself out. Kansas City coach Marv Levy had once commented with admiration that "Delaney works too hard." And if work was an addiction for Delaney, Kansas City coaches were feeding his habit by running the little back as often as 29 times in a game. As a result, little Joe's bones, especially his ribs, had barely made it through two seasons. With some more careful treatment, however, the "fastest back in the NFL" was sure to light up television sets with his electrifying runs.

Although nearly 100 miles from his home at Haughton, Delaney felt at ease in Monroe, where he often traveled to visit friends. As he sat, enjoying the unfamiliar role of spectator to the flurry of play around him, he noticed three boys playing in a large water hole. Construction workers had dug the pit to get the dirt they needed to build a giant water slide on the other side of the park. Since then heavy rains had fallen, turning the ditch into a lake. There were no safety fences to keep anyone out of the water, and it made Delaney nervous to watch the boys. With a new pit like that there was no telling where a drop-off might be.

Delaney yelled a warning to them, advising them to be careful not to wade too far into the water. But moments later the boys stepped off a submerged ledge into water far over their heads.

Joe Delaney had never learned how to swim. Yet he didn't hesitate a moment before charging across the grass and plunging into the treacherous, muddy water. Bursting out of nowhere to save the day was something that Delaney managed to do almost routinely. Before he arrived in Kansas City, the Chiefs had gone almost a decade without a winning season. Their running attack had been more a retreat than an attack. In 1980 Ted McKnight had been the only Chief to run for more than 300 yards. But the man who had been slotted as McKnight's backup had sprinted on to the scene to help the club to a first-place tie late in the season, and to finish only one game out of the play-offs. The cries for help that Delaney was answering in Monroe were far more desperate than those of Chiefs' fans and so he refused to waste even a fraction of a second. Adding a further handicap to his weak swimming skills, Delaney dove in fully clothed.

The two larger boys were in the worst trouble, and Delaney somehow managed to fish one of them out and pull him onto shore. The younger boy also scrambled his way back to safety but that still left one boy missing. Delaney dove back in to get him. Somewhere in that murky water, hands outstretched to find an 11-year-old boy and give him another chance at life, Joe Delaney's soul left this earth.

The futility of the effort was magnified by the fact that two of the boys he had tried to save eventually died in the accident. Delaney left behind a wife, three girls, ages seven years, five years, and four months, and a host of friends and acquaintances shocked and saddened that such a good man had been taken from them. They were shocked, not only by the sudden wrenching loss but also by the irony that a man who had always astounded people with his athletic gifts had never learned the one relatively common physical skill that he needed at that moment.

Delaney had built a career on the strength and efficiency of his body, and that had failed him in the end.

But the greater part of his success had been built on something more, on courage and selflessness. That had not failed him. When a former coach was told of the circumstance of Delaney's death he said without a trace of doubt, "He'd do it 100 times." Of all the high praise and glory that top athletes reap every day, it may be that none has ever earned and received a finer tribute than that.

Read John 15:13 for a final tribute to Joe Delaney.